Lost Vampire

Bit-Lit Series, Volume 1

W.J. May

Published by Dark Shadow Publishing, 2015.

This is a work of fiction. Similarities to real people, places, or events are entirely coincidental.

LOST VAMPIRE

First edition. November 18, 2015.

Copyright © 2015 W.J. May.

Written by W.J. May.

Also by W.J. May

Bit-Lit Series
Lost Vampire
Cost of Blood

Blood Red Series
Courage Runs Red
The Night Watch

Daughters of Darkness: Victoria's Journey
Huntress
Coveted (A Vampire & Paranormal Romance)
Victoria

Hidden Secrets Saga
Seventh Mark - Part 1
Seventh Mark - Part 2
Marked By Destiny
Compelled
Fate's Intervention
Chosen Three

The Chronicles of Kerrigan
Rae of Hope
Dark Nebula
House of Cards
Royal Tea
Under Fire
End in Sight

The Hidden Secrets Saga

Seventh Mark (part 1 & 2)

The Senseless Series
Radium Halos
Radium Halos - Part 2
Nonsense

Standalone
Shadow of Doubt (Part 1 & 2)
Five Shades of Fantasy
Glow - A Young Adult Fantasy Sampler
Shadow of Doubt - Part 2
Four and a Half Shades of Fantasy
Full Moon
Dream Fighter
What Creeps in the Night
Forest of the Forbidden
HuNted
Arcane Forest: A Fantasy Anthology
Ancient Blood of the Vampire and Werewolf

Lost Vampire
Book 1 of The Bit-Lit Series
BY
W.J. May
Copyright 2015 by W.J. May

All rights reserved. No part of this publication may be reproduced, stored in or introduced into a retrieval system, or transmitted, in any form, or by any means (electronic, mechanical, photocopying, recording, or otherwise) without the prior written permission of both the copyright owner and the above publisher of this book. This is a work of fiction. Names, characters, places, brands, media, and incidents are either the product of the author's imagination or are used fictitiously. Any resemblance to actual person, living or dead, events, or locales is entirely coincidental. The author acknowledges the trademarked status and trademark owners of various products referenced in this work of fiction, which have been used without permission. The publication/use of these trademarks is not authorized, associated with, or sponsored by the trademark owners.

All rights reserved.
Copyright 2015 by W.J. May

No part of this book may be used or reproduced in any manner whatsoever without written permission, except in the case of brief quotations embodied in articles and reviews.

Bit Lit Series:

Lost Vampire - Book 1
Cost of Blood – Book 2
Book 3
Coming January 2016

W.J. May Info:

Website: http://www.wanitamay.yolasite.com
Facebook: https://www.facebook.com/pages/Author-WJ-May-FAN-PAGE/141170442608149
SIGN UP FOR **W.J. May's Newsletter** to find out about new releases, updates, cover reveals and even freebies!
http://eepurl.com/97aYf

LOST VAMPIRE

Lost Vampire – Description

The future is not a safe place. When Tay Maslov was a girl, she lived in New York State, and her playground were the sun-drenched fields of her parent's farm. But all that changed when one day the Servitors came, looking for new recruits for their master, the Archon Jeremiah of Brooklyn.

The vampires – or Elders – rule the cities now, and hardly any humans are left out in the wildernesses. All of that land is given over to the weird animal-like Shifters. The Elders run the Blood Banks, enforced Blood Donations, as well as the Blood Clubs, and the culls of insurgents. When Tay Maslov, many years later and now a vampire herself, servant to her Archon Jeremiah, refuses to go on a cull of the poor humans she is cast down, become a Feral; hated by all. It is in this state that she meets Kaiden, himself a creature of the night – but far different from her.

Which of them will survive what comes next?

1. Tay, Dreaming

"From where they originally came, no one knows – or perhaps is allowed to know – but there are several sources we can refer to. The Chronicles of Tancred in the 11th century retell the story of the 'Lych Papacy' and the beginnings of the Cursed Crusades to try to unseat them. By then, however, the vampires were already a sizeable community. Perhaps the stories from afar are correct, and that they are indeed a different species of human, or near-human, been with us, preying on us since the very beginning of time... By the time of the Late Renaissance however, their grip over the development of our mortal, sun-loving society was complete."

- *The Helsing Talks (BANNED)*

Rain. Dark streets are washed with the fragments of reflected neon light, and Tabitha Maslov has got that muzzy sort of headache behind her eyes, like a hangover. The problem is that she hasn't been drinking. Tabitha Maslov, or Tay, hadn't been *dreaming* in a while. That is to say, the young woman with the bedraggled dark hair and short jacket hadn't been out *hunting*. It's the mortals who call it that, *dreaming*, a term for the dark and dreadful state of feverish nightmares that they fall into as soon as a being such as her starts to feed on a live human.

Tabitha Maslov, perennially late, with her mussed hair and barely enough money in her pocket to pay her rent, is one of the Dark Kindred. The Elders. A vampire.

And if she doesn't get something to eat soon, she'll start to starve.

"Feral." The sneer hurt more than the slap that had followed it as Tay Maslov stood in front of her superior and leader, the fair-haired, pale-faced Archon Jeremiah Worthington.

Jeremiah was one of the four Archons of the City of New York, each overseeing their own circles of vampire brood in each district. Until just recently, Tabitha had been a resident of Jeremiah's district and forced to report her activities to him every moon-cycle. It was a harsh society that the Elders had created for their subordinates; both the established, older kindred and the younger neonates like Tabitha Maslov.

But, as the vampire saying goes, the world is built on blood.

Each Archon has not only his own kindred to oversee, but also the relations with the mortal counsels under their protection as well. There are constant squabbles as the human officials start to complain that there are too many *dreamers* in their neighbourhood or quarter, and that they must be given some respite from the relentless hunger of their elders. Archon Jeremiah, in particular, was known to be a hard negotiator, and he cared little for the desires of the humans that he saw merely as slaves.

"I name you *Feral* before the eyes of your circle, your brood, and your city." Jeremiah's words were cold, like his crystal-clear blue eyes, like drops of lake ice in white skin. He wore his fair hair straight and long past his shoulders, and a formal brocade coat of scintillating crimsons, red flower designs, silk and cotton. Jeremiah was taller than Tay by a good six inches, his high cheekbones and forehead displaying the traditional contours of the European vampire lines from which he had been sired.

But it's all a stupid affectation, Tay thought, her own sneer loud in her mind but quiet on her tongue. *Our beloved Archon is only what, a hundred and fifty years old? Two hundred at a push?* The pale girl thought to herself. Archon Jeremiah was one of the youngest of the four Archons that controlled the metropolitan area of New York. He had gotten to his current rank by a mixture of unbelievable bad luck on the part of his own sire (the bad luck being that he was found bound to a concrete culvert as the sun came up), and to his ability to ingratiate himself with the other Archons, providing favours, money, or allies whenever they required.

The problem with Archon Jeremiah, Tay saw, was that he was still a small fish in a big pond. He wore re-created dress suits some hundreds of years old, and carried replica rapiers and duelling pistols to ape the older Archons.

He must want so desperately to fit in. Tay felt the side of her mouth twitch.

Unfortunately for Tay, however, if Jeremiah was still a small fish, then she must be at the level of plankton in vampire society – and the humans that they shepherded as unknown and uncountable as the drops of water they swam in.

"How dare you!" Jeremiah's voice spat, just a second before his long-fingered hand delivered another ringing slap, this time on the other side of her face where her smile had almost been.

Tay felt her eyes burning, but whether with tears or in anger she couldn't tell. The slap itself didn't really hurt, all vampires – even the youngest, fifty-year-old neonates such as her had a re-knit skin, tendon, and bone structure that made them tough by normal mortal standards.

"Did you think that I wouldn't find out?" Jeremiah said.

Tay opened her mouth to speak, about to shake her head – but she knew that it was no use. The Archon's word was final, and he had no intention of listening to a mere neonate's protestations.

"Word was brought to me that you have not been performing your duties for the good of the city. That there are insurgents operating in your neighbourhood."

"What-" Tay started to protest. This was the first that she had ever heard *that* particular accusation.

"*And*, when I call upon *all* of my neonates to participate in a cull of their areas of the city, and to deliver the criminal goods found, why do you refuse?"

Tay's hands clenched as she remembered what had happened. The culls of the mortal inhabitants of the cities were being called with more and more frequency across the city. They were always a messy, brutal affair, as the neonates and their human servitors went door-to-door, apartment-to-apartment, block-by-block to search for signs of the insurgent human rebels and their sacrilegious, criminal artifacts. Those found with rebellious tracts and manuscripts, or with secret idols or weapons capable of killing a vampire, were taken for further 'questioning' before being culled. Usually, in order to make up the numbers needed for the reports, men and women who only had the most spurious connection to the vigilante insurgents that had seeded themselves into the city over the last decade were taken in for questioning:. a mother who had a rebellious son, or a school-teacher who had once taught a pupil who, years later, was caught in an insurgent cell.

On this latest cull, Tabitha had opted to 'disappear' for the night of blood-letting, screams, and terror. The Archon's servitors had found her in a small basement Blood-Bar, where pale-skinned, ghoulish humans talked and smoked and listened to dreamy, fatalistic music.

It wasn't the first time that Tabitha had missed a cull, but it appeared that it was today that the Archon had decided to make an example out of her.

"If you have no stomach for the clean-up of your neighbourhood, then I would suggest that you spend a few months finding out what life is like for those who have *no* neighbourhood. You will be outcast from your brood and our circle. No other Elder will shelter you, nor will they provide you with food," Jeremiah said with a savage smile. "You shall have no rights to the blood banks, and you shall have no standing in Elder society. You will be Feral, for a period of my choosing – and if you are alive at the end of it, then we shall see if you have reconsidered your duties and responsibilities to your city."

Feral. Even the word made Tabitha shudder. Aside from outright criminal conviction and punishment, it was the worst fate that vampire society could impose. It meant that she would have no immediate access to the blood banks that the Elders forced the humans to donate to. Nor could she attend the blood-bars and practice her *dreaming* directly on a live, willing human donor. No other vampire in Elder society could give her a place to rest, or succour of any kind.

The young woman with the dark hair thought of the other Ferals she had seen; half-mad, savage creatures that existed in the cracks of Elder society, living in the sewers and hunting the homeless humans they shared their space with. Or, wandering from hotel to hotel, perennially getting attacked by other Elders as they sought willing donors on luck and instinct alone.

Many started to succumb to the blood-madness if they didn't *dream* regularly. Their bodies became starved of blood, and the vampiric virus that had taken over their bodies started to infect their brains, making them relive every primordial horror that was pregnant in their veins. Eventually, if they hadn't fed in a long while, they became creatures of the virus alone – incapable of rational society, and just predatory beasts that were rounded up at the same time as the human insurgents during the culls.

Tabitha felt, for perhaps the first time in a long while, a new, shuddering sensation in her chest. She felt *fear*.

"Why was I so stupid?" Tay muttered to herself as she lurched. Her feet felt heavy, as if she were wading through glue, and the wet, slick paving stones of the street below her seemed to waver in and out of focus.

I should have just gone to the cull. She leaned against the pull-down metal barricade of a shop window for support. It was night time, of course, and this was a quiet part of town. Many mortals chose to not go out at night at all – those who were the most reserved and frightened of their Elder overseers. Tay, however, was banking on the fact that she might be able to find some Blood Dolls or Blood Brothers, out for a party and seeking an Elder to offer their 'services' to.

Warm. Even just the thought of the fresh blood made her stomach cramp in hunger, and the nerves behind her eyes throb with pain. She'd already gone a week without feeding, staying in her louse-ridden apartment (the only one that she could afford now that all of her standing in the community had been revoked) and hoping for the Archon's servitors to knock on the door and ask if she had learnt her lesson.

The hunger had finally driven her to the streets.

It was the strange vampiric virus inside of her, she knew, but Tay always believed that it was also alive in a way that was far beyond the mere remit of a virus. *It's my curse*, she thought. *My shadow. A dark spirit sitting inside of me.* Her feet slipped on the concrete as another pain shot through her muscles. What made it worse was that Tay hadn't felt anything like serious pain for a long while now. She knew discomfort, tiredness, but sensations like cold and warm had become mere annoyances.

And what sort of sodding virus makes it impossible to be seen on video? She cursed inwardly. It was true: vampiric bodies exerted some subtle aura of electromagnetic interference, making any attempt to digitally capture them result in fuzzy, ghostly images of half-formed ghouls. Of course, many people believed that this was none other than the real monster inside of the Elders being captured, but modern science disapproved of this speculation.

This interference was also blamed for many of the feelings that mortals have around vampires: the sense of prickling on their skin, the unease that they feel for no reason, other than the fact that the person they might be talking to doesn't even have to breathe in order to stay alive. Of course, nothing that science had found could explain the other strangest of symptoms that the vampire species displayed: an uncanny ability to sense danger, to read others' minds – there was even talk of vampires that could move objects just with the power of their minds.

Scientists blamed the vampiric virus as it slowly spread into the central brain stem of its host, re-awakening and mutating every nerve cluster that it came into contact with.

Tay, however, thought that the old superstitions were right. They were all cursed; the descendants of Cain, doomed to wander the earth forever without succour or support from the righteous.

There was a tinkle of smashing glass and a giggle of laughter from up ahead. Tay felt her knees give way as pain lanced through them. She hit the alleyway like a cast-away marionette, her palms slapping the ground. Sensation was starting to tingle up into her arms.

So weak, weak! She shook, looking up as a couple emerged from the head of the alleyway.

A young couple, pale skin, dressed in black with the powder-white face of their kind: a Blood Doll and Blood Brother, young, probably drunk.

"Please... Help me..." Tay reached out her hands towards them, meaning to bargain for the nourishment that only they could give. All that came out, however, was a high, keening, rasping noise like an injured bird.

Her pupils were starting to dilate, overlaying the image of the couple ahead with suddenly sharp, bright details: the strands of dyed-black hair tucked behind the woman's ear. The glint of the small Ankh that the earlobe held.

"Holy crap, Ryan! There's someone down there!" she heard the Doll say.

They smelled of harsh alcohol and cigarette smoke. They must have been at a Blood-Bar or a club not far from here, a couple of the eternal groupies who tried to track down the Elders and offer them their blood, in the hopes of becoming a servitor in Elder society (and maybe, just possibly, even allowed to turn into a full-blooded Kindred).

Tay Maslov had been one of those pale young things once, many years ago.

Too young and too stupid to know what I was doing. All I saw was the beauty and the elegance, the strength and the courage. Tay's body was starting to shiver and shake where it lay on the ground.

The Blood Dolls and Brothers were looked down on by the Elders, a pleasurable but rather pathetic attempt by some mortals to come to terms with their fate. Ever since the Elders had first risen to prominence, it had been this way – there had been humans who were more than willing to throw themselves into their dark embrace.

"Celestina... can you feel it? It's... it's one of *them*," the boy was saying. Some of his white face-powder had become smeared, and Tay could smell the salty tang of sweat on his brow. A part of the vampire laughed – the small, still-sane part that was always watching. These Dolls always conjured up ridiculous names like Celestina or Vlad for themselves, as if there weren't already a few thousand Alucards and Suspiras in the city alone.

Tay opened her mouth to beg just for a little taste, but all that came out was more keening. The vision of the two grew closer, in fits and starts, as she must have faded in and out of consciousness.

I wonder if this is what death feels like. Nothing. Just pure nothing, Tay wondered, shaking.

In another few flashes, the young girl, stinking of cheap perfume and vodka, was kneeling over her, with the boy looking over his shoulder fearfully. Even though the Elders were in charge, it was still technically looked down upon to feed a Feral.

Usually these arrangements were done in private, with lots of money.

"Are you sure you want to do this?" the boy was saying, his voice morphing strangely in Tay's fever-ridden ears.

The girl was leaning down close, and Tabitha could feel the warmth of her breath on her hair. Soothing, cooling hands were on the back of her neck, massaging under her hairline.

"She needs help, Ryan. She needs us," the girl, Celestina was saying, shuffling Tabitha's head onto the lap of her faded black denim jeans, cut and scored many times to reveal the smooth thighs beneath.

Tabitha was starting to shiver, her hands making useless grabbing motions with no strength.

There was a movement, a sudden intake of breath. A private gasp of pain from the girl, then a white forearm presented itself in front of Tay, a small nick on the side already welling with fresh blood.

Tabitha didn't need to be offered twice, but she was too weak to take it. The arm was pushed gently against her lips, and she started to drink.

Salty. Bitter. The heavy taste of iron – and – *life!*

Whatever it is that the vampires produce when they feed, whether it a secret chemical in their saliva or really their dark enchantment, it started to happen between Tabitha and the unknown girl. A sensation like standing at the edge of a cliff rushed over Tay, invigorating her, making her fingers and toes curl. Above her there was an accompanying sigh from the girl as they both, in their own way, started to *dream*.

The rush of blood to a vampire brings new life, and the promise of every good, strong thing that they could have been or have yet to become. Some vampires feel themselves to be invincible when *dreaming*, others experience the most intense, private moments of bliss and satisfaction. For every vampire it is different, answering the call of their heart and needs in a different way. It is no wonder that the act of feeding is regarded as a sacred act to many Elders. It is their panacea to their dark existence.

For Tay:

She remembers running her hand over green sheaths of sweetcorn, many, many years before coming to where she is now. She is young still – just a teenage girl, a smattering of years before she decides to leave home, move to the city, and start wearing the black of a Blood Doll.

Back then – now – she regarded her rural New York State life in a small farm tucked under the mountains as backwards, uncouth, uncivilised. She didn't realize why her parents forbade her to come to the city when they went to the monthly blood collections. Her parents never had joined the ranks of the Dolls and Brothers enamoured of their Elder overlords. Her parents just raised few crops, and tried to force their only daughter to spend as much time as possible in the sunlight of their farm and the greenish twilight of the mountains' forest above their home; every hour of every day, a paean to summer, daylight, and the sun.

It was almost as if her parents had known that a dark fascination was already growing inside their little girl; that one day she would seek the riches, glory, and shadowed splendour of the Elders.

In her alleyway, Tabitha guzzled and drank, drenching herself in memories.

For now, however, little Tabitha Maslov was happy. Her parents' plan seemed to be working; she was being inoculated against the night with the seduction of summer. All around her the corn was growing, their long, papery leaves a brilliant viridian and soft under her touch. It must have been late spring or early summer, as they were still only a few feet high. The younger Tabitha Maslov liked to walk between the rows when they were at this stage, feeling like a giant, feeling surrounded by growing things.

A fat bee the size of her thumb waggled its way over the heads of corn, before disappearing into the glare of the sun. Tay felt her skin flush with warmth, her ears full of the whooping sound of a far-off forest bird.

For a moment, Tabitha felt complete.

There is a sound like a whimper above her, and a shudder. For a moment, Tay is once again in the dark, wet, dirty alleyway with the unknown girl. Only this time, the girl's other arm is around her back and her fingers are kneading the firm muscles of her shoulders. Whatever the human Celestina is experiencing, it isn't the same as Tay. The human girl appears to crave the sensation of *dreaming* as much as Tay does, but not because it brings life. Instead it is an addiction. A rush.

But Tay submerges again into the dream.

There is warmth all around her, and her skin feels something. It feels the flow of air against it, the slack relaxedness of well-worked muscles. Tay feels alive again.

The Tabitha-in-the-past turns to call out to her parents; parents she hasn't seen in many years now, who probably died many decades ago. A part of Tabitha knows what must have happened – that when she moved from Blood Doll to full-blooded Elder, she must have disappeared from their life. Their attempts to track down their daughter would have returned only dead-ends, polite but forceful refusals. Eventually, strange and pale-suited servitors would have knocked on their door, delivering the news that their daughter was now dead.

It was an open secret what this meant. That their daughter had either had the misfortune to die in a 'complication' during a feeding, or that she had committed one of the many crimes that the Elders had defined for mortal society. Or, perhaps, the smallest chance of all, that she had become a Servitor or even an Elder. As the many centuries had taught the mortals, any further investigation or willingness to track down their missing relative would result in their 'disappearing' too.

The Tabitha who was now was lost forever to them.

The Tabitha-in-the-past still had a chance to see them, to talk one last time to her parents, even if they were only dream-parents. The girl turns in the field, her sneakers crunching in the dirt and dried earth below.

The glare from the sun is bright. Too bright. So bright that it hurts her eyes even.

The Tabitha-in-the-past opens her mouth, but all that comes out is a thin, high-pitched keening. She is shocked, but not shaken. In fact, a sense of electricity is running through her veins.

Something is wrong.

Tay opens her eyes to the alleyway, to find the voices loud and alien all around her, her vision swimming in and out of focus.

"What...?" She tried to stand, to push herself off of the ground but she can't. Her limbs feel rubbery and made of jelly.

I've been drugged! The thought sears through her mind like a dart. Even though vampires were technically immortal and immune to most mortal diseases and illnesses, they could still be drugged by the use of a willing (and unscreened) Blood Doll. Even heavy intoxication like spirits and recreational drugs could pass on a slight effect to vampires through the dream – which is why the Blood Banks exist, to screen and purify all of the donations brought in. The Elders who went to the Blood Bars for 'live meat' usually demanded to see a screening card to verify that their donor had been tested recently.

What Tay was feeling now wasn't just the effects of passed-on, second-hand alcohol. Not even most narcotics. She blinked her eyes groggily, feeling worse than she had before she had fed.

"Get her arms," Ryan was saying, his voice at once deafeningly loud and like a buzzing gnat.

Tay succeeded in rolling over onto her side. At some point, Celestina must have disengaged herself –quite a feat, given that she looked to be in the pitch, swell, and throws of excitement.

They must have planned this, the vampire thought, opening her mouth to shout, but only succeeding in moaning loudly. Every part of her body felt stiff and alien to her, far away.

Rough hands grabbed her ankles, and she tried to kick, but her legs didn't seem to want to obey her right now. Two more pinched her arms, and she saw the flash of dark hair. Celestina.

"Nnnngh..!" Tay managed to thrash slightly, rolling out of their grasp.

"Give it up, leech!" The man's voice was angry, followed by a sharp prod in her back. "We're not going to stake you...*yet.*" It was followed by a rough laugh. "There's someone who wants to see one of you up close."

"Fghngh!" Tay started to growl, managing to land a half-decent scratch on the girl, Celestina.

"Ugh! You little..." Celestina jumped backward, holding her arm that was now a mess of freshly-spilt red. She didn't look like the amorous, needy Blood Doll anymore. If Tay hadn't been so hungry, she was sure that she would have noticed the healthy glow of muscles under the girl's top, the confidant, athletic way that she held herself.

"You've had enough outta me, blood-sucker," Celestina hissed at the crouching Tay. "When we're through with you, I'll cut off your head personally." She grinned, and it was wicked and full of fervour.

Tay tried to stand. If she were well, she would be more than a match for mortals – even ones with apparent physical training. Tay would have had the advantage of speed, strength, and the inability to feel minor pain or fatigue. That is, *if* she were well, but she wasn't. Once again, her knees gave way and she found herself wallowing in the dirty diesel-water of the alleyway.

"Hah!" the man – 'Ryan' – laughed, stepping forward once more.

"Back off!" There was a shout, and a shadow passed in front of her eyes, accompanied by a dull thumping noise.

Tay tried to open her eyes, but all she could see were sudden flashes of movement and light. She heard the gargled sound of a scream, grunts, and running footsteps. There was a moment of silence, and then she felt a shadow fall over her once again. She was looking at the silhouette of a male form, dark, rough brown hair falling over his shadowed green eyes.

"Help..." Tay tried to whisper. She couldn't get an accurate read on the figure through the fog of her illness. Was he another of her attackers? A mortal? He wore dark, tight clothing built more for speed and comfort: Dark combat trousers and flexible mountain boots, and a loose urban jacket with reinforced shoulders, elbows, and anachronistic brass buttons.

"Hmm," he grunted as he knelt over Tay. "You've been poisoned. It's a new drug on the streets. With any luck, we can get you somewhere safe before they come back with their friends."

"Friends..?" Tay coughed, wincing as she felt strong hands under her knees and behind her back, lifting her in one smooth movement. She caught a glimpse out of the corner of her eye of one outstretched, pale arm lying on the ground. The mortal, Ryan, was otherwise unmoving.

"Yeah. You're not the first one who's been at the wrong end of them." His voice was light, but mature, and he spoke like he was used to this sort of situation.

"But-but. Not the Sanctuary. I can't. Can't..." Tay tried to force the words through her stubborn lips that she was Feral, and that meant that no Elder would take her in.

There was a dry chuckle from the man as he carried her out of the alleyway. "Don't worry; I don't really think that they would let someone like me in there anyway."

Tay saw streetlights, and the familiar sound of far-off cars in the city. She felt sick, but curiosity still consumed her.

"Bruh-brood..?" she tried to inquire, certain that the man who was seemingly saving her must be an Elder.

The man, however, remained silent for a moment. "Kaiden. That's my name. I guess you could say I am a brood all of my own."

Hope of a kindred spirit sparked in the vampire. Maybe he was like her. "Fuh... Fuh... Feral?"

Silence, again.

His steps were quick as he shifted her in his arms, stopping for a moment to help her to stand. Tay re-focused her aching eyes to see a dark car like a sort of small 4X4, dark, with tinted windows. There was the sound of doors being unlocked, and she was being slid onto the backseat, before he went around the other way to hop in the driver's side.

"Okay, you just hang on tight there for a moment, and we'll get you somewhere you can rest up..." Kaiden was saying, but Tay was already succumbing to darkness.

Tabitha Maslov slept.

She remembers hands holding her neck, strong, warm hands lifting her head to a plastic bag of blood; the kind that the Elders can claim at the Blood Banks. Kaiden must have used his own rations or Servitors to get one, and now he is giving it to her. Before Tay could thank him, she is submerged once more in the *dream*, golden fields, warm, dappled sunlight in the leaves, a hint of laughter as they played by the lake...

The next thing Tay remembers is waking up to find herself in a large warehouse-like apartment, the top floor of a redevelopment block maybe. There're wide windows along one complete side of the wall, and a mattress underneath her, on the floor. The smell of turpentine and chemicals. Oddly-matched bits of furniture clustering about a stand, where half a dozen canvases sit, half-finished. Before she can try to see what they are, she is falling into the nothingness of sleep again.

Snatches of wakefulness. Heavy blinds pulled over the windows, the hazy glow of the covered sun filtering through.

Guttural voices at the door of the apartment. "No. Nowhere near ready. It can't be done," a voice, Kaiden, saying.

"We thought we could trust you, man!" another answers, and then blackness.

Kaiden's face, lit up by the streetlights below. Quick, hawkish features. Dark eyebrows, his green eyes covered in shadow. A highlight of yellow neon light walking down one cheek. He is sitting on the open windowsill of his apartment, musing, frowning, thinking about something as he looks at the dirty city below.

Then darkness. Sleep. The memory of sunlight.

2. Kaiden, Hunting

"From the earliest days, there have been tales of monsters in the dark places. Wolves in the forest, trolls in the mountains. Now we know that our ancestors were always correct. The Shifters were always with us..."

- *The Helsing Talks (BANNED)*

The light hurt his eyes, but he still had to go out. Kaiden found a snarl trying to rise in the back of his throat, but he swallowed it, forced it down.

No. Not now. The man knew that there was no time for that now. No time for the hunt, or for the chorus of rage that bellowed for blood in his heart. *Would it always be like this? Always?* He felt his stomach lurch with the immensity of his undertaking. *Will I always have to feel like this...so angry all the time? So hungry?*

Kaiden was a young man by any standard, to the Elders and humans alike. He was only just into his twenties, and that was all. The girl he had rescued last night – she only appeared nineteen, but he knew that she was older. Not *very* old, maybe only forty or fifty or so, but she still had a paleness to her skin that betrayed the fact that her body was extending its life unnaturally.

All of the Elders became like that in the end, the man thought, shaking his head as another wave of anger threatened to unseat him.

No. Keep focused. Remember the techniques, Kaiden told himself, forcing himself to go through the breathing exercises that his mentor had once taught him before he left the apartment. It only took a few moments to restore his heart rate to its regular over-a-hundred patter. Normal for what he was, he guessed.

Looking around, he could see that the girl was asleep on the mattress, rolled over from the dull glow of dirty sunlight filtering through the heavy blinds. The Elders couldn't stand sunlight, and the older they grew, the more it had a toxic effect on them. At her age, it would probably just produce a skin rash and pain, but it was said that the oldest of her kind, the European Conclave, might spontaneously catch fire if put in front of sunlight.

And oh, what joy that would be! Kaiden grinned to himself at the thought, before unbolting the door and sweeping out of it. The door closed on an automatic locking mechanism as soon as he left – the most expensive thing about the whole place, as he was renting it unofficially, giving some money to a man named Baker, the building's manager, in return for keeping the developers away.

Kaiden found himself in the familiar dirty corridor and metal stairs that zigzagged one side of the warehouse complex. Plastic bags, half-rotten newspapers, and bits of even more undistinguishable refuse crunched underfoot. Kaiden was tall for his age, with dark hair shaved at the sides that fell over his deeply shadowed eyes if he let it. He wore a shabby reinforced urban jacket with brass buttons – the only holdover of his previous life, and finished off the outfit with dark chinos and combat boots. It made him look like the rougher end of the spectrum of urban mortal, but acceptable. No one would take him for what he really was.

Abomination. Servant. Slave.

The words skittered across the young man's mind as quick as a whisper, and his hands tensed, his heartrate started to rise; he could feel a stab of a headache as his pupils suddenly dilated. The corridor and the stairs drew into sharp focus, with the flies and the earwigs pricked out in crystal-clear detail.

"Hey, bro – hey man, spare us a dime..." Someone lurched out of one of the doors at the top of the next landing. Industrial techno music with a glitch-step beat swam around him, almost deafening his still-adjusting ears. It was one of the other degenerates from a few floors below, jumping out to beg or steal some money from any of the other unaffected, illegal tenants who stayed in Baker's warehouse block. The guy had half of his head shaved, and the other half dyed platinum white in fallen-over spikes. A pair of goggles and a waistcoat over a bare, pale chest completed the image.

Freak. Monster. Slave.

Kaiden turned around, snarling at the man, seeing the poor guy gasp in almost slow motion – his own eyes widening in fear, sweat popping up on his skin; a smell of fear-sweat filling the stairwell instantly.

"Holy crap!" the guy uttered, falling backwards into his apartment.

Damn. Kaiden gritted his teeth, feeling the incisors sitting against his lower jaw as he started to clatter down the stairs. Hopefully the guy would think it was just a nightmare – some delirious vision of whatever drink or drugs he was putting into his body. Hopefully.

Kaiden hit the bottom of the stairs, took a deep breath, and plunged into the pool of watery light from the open door to the street outside. He wondered what he would be forced to do if the guy *did* remember what had happened, and started talking about it to his friends...

The weak sunlight flooded his eyes as he stepped out of the warehouse, causing him to wince. He must have spent too long indoors again. Either that, or his modified eyes were starting the process of reacting to the sun. Bright, lightning flashes across the back of his eyeballs as the photons sear their way through his already dark, enlarged pupils. Even in this day and age of restricted light and heavy UV filtering enforced by the Elders, the light still hurt someone like him...

Abomination. Freak. Monster...

The youth's head rang with the words that the old man had said. *Not him. Anyone but him!* Kaiden remembered thinking, looking around for any support, any friendship in the room at all.

The cold eyes and the fearful snarls from the Shifters were all that he was offered. Everyone here in this room, everyone standing in a semi-circle in front of him, thought the same thing. He was now no longer Kaiden Ottaker; he was something else.

"What have you done, you old fool?" snarled the tallest among them, clothed in russet, and with dark, tangled hair. That would be Lubok, the largest Shifter and local pack leader. Kaiden had looked up to him once, when they had first met – but it had always been a fearful admiration, as the Shifter was only ever half-civilised, and he treated all of those around him as his personal servants.

"No – no, it cannot be..." the old man said, and Kaiden felt his heart breaking. If Professor Williams could say that, then it must be true.

"No. It was a mistake. Get the lights," Lubok snarled, and the other Shifters around quickly turned, flipping the switches on the UV floodlights that they had brought especially for this purpose.

Bright, glaring light filled Kaiden's eyes, blinding him, burning him.

He howled.

"We have to kill it! It was a mistake!" Lubok was shouting as Kaiden thrashed, feeling his limbs cramp as adrenaline and stranger chemicals coursed through them. He couldn't see, and he felt pain lancing through him as the light started to take its toll. He was confused.

Why are they treating me like this? Why, when I have done everything they told me to? More importantly – why was Professor Williams, the man who had taken him in when the Elders had killed his parents and had kept him safe for the past three years, agreeing with them? Surely the Professor knew that underneath all of this he was still Kaiden...

Kaiden screamed again, and it came out like a pained, hissing, snarling sound. He was on the floor, writhing in agony. He didn't remember when he had fallen down, but he had. He lashed out with his hands and feet, hearing the medical tables and scientific instruments crash around him.

"You're right. He's a monster. An abomination," he heard the Professor say faintly, sadly.

That was when the rage blossomed inside him, and he lost who he was, or who he had ever been, for a time. How could the Professor say that to him? How could he do that to him?

The light was everywhere, and it was blinding. It had made Kaiden mad. He remembered little of what transpired, apart from blood and screams.

Back in the present, the young man blinked the tears out of his eyes, blaming the light, always blaming the light. Shaking his head, he pushed on through the umbral city, using the back-lanes and access roads, the cross-sections and alleyways to get to where he was going.

The river. Where the human markets were. He could hear them even before he drew close, a churning roil of human activity; of shouts and screams – even of laughter. The mortals were desperate to live every second they had away from the tyranny of light.

The markets had taken hold since the uprisings a generation ago, when large parts of the city were set ablaze by insurgents seeking to fire the hiding places, vaults, and sleeping crypts of the Elders. They had failed, of course, but they had left behind them burnt-out buildings and half-demolished streets. Once all of the bodies were cleared away, and the servitors of the Elders established their rule once again, the mortals slowly drifted back to this area, setting up wooden market stalls, stringing colourful cloth covers from the ruins, organizing small, ad-hoc lanes through the rubble.

The markets became a place of resistance, but not of an armed kind. Instead, it was a resistance of activity – of buying, selling, haggling and *being* human, and not just the fearful things that the Elders made of them.

The Elders let them have their markets; as long as the Servitors were always watching during the day, what harm could it do? They cracked down every few years, sending in teams to demand taxation or blood tribute, but mostly they left the mortals to their semblance of life. Whilst they were shopping to survive, they weren't plotting or organising.

At least, that was what Kaiden assumed of the Elders. Maybe it was all some elaborate scheme in their generations-long strategy.

The man shook his head, shrugging his ignorance away, and slipped into the crowds of people that walked the streets between the stalls. Instantly, he was surrounded by the sights and smells of humanity. Coffee roasting. Spices the people hand-picked and sold direct to customers. Vegetables grown in hydroponic laboratories. Tobacco. Colourful garments.

Above him, the fetid sky looked pale compared to the brightly dyed and painted canvas awnings. The sky was a yellow-grey haze, a heavy day for the 'Solar Stability' programme that was gradually transforming their planet into a dismal, darkened haze.

"Yeah, boy, they got the factories working overtime today, ain't they?" an old timer cackled and spat on the broken paving stones underfoot. He had obviously just seen Kaiden looking up at the darkening sky above.

"Hmm," Kaiden agreed, unsure of what to say – if anything. The towers that the Elders situated wherever they went were always churning out, night and day, the tall white plumes that the mortals were told were occluding their atmosphere. It was hard for Kaiden to fathom it, that it was even possible for such a technology to exist, or that the human mortals had ever put up with it. It seemed all like a surreal nightmare, from which no one could ever wake up.

Had the sky got perceptibly darker since he was a child? Were the summers getting less bright? Kaiden found it hard to tell; if there was a change, it was so gradual that he couldn't say for sure.

And therein lies their advantage, he thought as he trudged first down an alleyway of stalls, and then another. The light *did* get gloomier down here, but only because there were more drapes and awnings across the sky now. He was near the centre of the crooked market itself. *The Elders. They have the advantage of time. How can we defeat beings that plan in centuries?*

His hyper-sensitive ears alerted him to the sound of approaching jangling, and his shoulders started to relax. He was here. He had made it.

"Mercy for the lost?" a low, grumbling voice said ahead of him.

Kaiden looked up to see an old woman, long white hair almost to her knees, wearing the black and ash-grey habits of one of the minor religious orders. She leaned heavily on a crutch, and her ankles and wrists were bound with tiny bells.

"We're all lost, sister," he replied, and a second later the older woman smiled a small, half-smile in response. Kaiden had given the appropriate code-word; he was allowed to continue.

"Come with me," she said, her voice losing a little of its crackle and instead taking on more of its more natural resonance. The woman's skin was tanned and deeply wrinkled, and Kaiden knew that this was due to the fact that she spent all of her time 'when not working as a guide for the insurgents' underground, under hydroponic sunlamps. A real Elder wouldn't be too affected by them, but the glare hurt.

It even hurts my eyes.

The Guide pushed aside a collection of heavy curtains, disrupting a small pyramid of chicken cages, each with their squawking resident. She pulled him beyond, deeper into the warren of stacked goods under fabric roofs or occasionally past the still-burnt, ruined walls of what buildings had once stood here. This part of the market was deeper and darker, and sold more curious items. Live animals. Charms against the Elders (they didn't work). Full lighting rigs (they did). Narcotics. Medicines.

Blood.

The smell hit Kaiden's nostrils the way that others meet coffee. His feet bunched, his steps staggered, and the Guide woman turned, her face looking wary, concerned.

"You haven't been dreaming, have you?" she said, accusatorily.

Kaiden shook his head. "I can't," he said, his voice thick.

"Hsss!" the woman made a screeching sound under her breath. "No wonder you're tottering like that! You *have* to! What do you think will happen, hmm?" She tapped him not too friendlily with the butt of her staff. "And when I knew it was you, I thought The Beast of New York had come to its senses."

"Stop it," Kaiden found himself growling. "Don't call me that."

"What?" the old woman snapped at him as she started to tug at the canvas around one of her particular stalls. "Why not? I'm the only one who will talk to you; you know that, don't you? Lubok and the others want to hunt you down."

"Maybe they should," Kaiden said as his eyes suddenly widened at the sight in front of him: Contraband blood packs, stolen from the banks by a worker friendly to the resistance. People like the Guide sister here distributed them to the Blood Dolls and Brothers, trying to wean them off of their habit and reduce the addiction that made the human mortals into servitors of the Elders.

And then there was Kaiden, of course.

"Don't give me that claptrap. We've been through this," the Guide sister snapped, pulling a purple-red blood pack from its semi-chilled case and handing it to him. "Don't ever forget who you are talking to, young man. I knew Professor Williams. I know what he sacrificed for you."

"I killed him," Kaiden said, his hands shaking as he held the blood pack in his hands.

"Shhh! Ain't no need to go over that again now!" the old woman snarled. "Now, I know that Williams had a plan when he asked you to do what you did – and you believed in him when you agreed."

"I thought that I would be helping the resistance. I didn't know that it would turn me into a monster..." Kaiden's voice was tired and thin. He had been over this so many times in the last two years.

"And neither did he, and he's dead and that's that," the old woman said with a sigh. "Now you've got to live with what you are, and make something of it. Starving yourself isn't going to help anyone, is it?"

"I-I need more," Kaiden said in a rush, trying to keep his eyes neutral, and not notice the way that the Guide sister looked at him. He knew that she was measuring him, assessing him, and thinking every moment: Is he turning the whole way? Will he do it right here and now? What if Lubok was right?

"More?" she said carefully, picking the word and placing it in the air between them. "I promised you that I would try to keep you alive until an answer for your *condition* appeared, but I never said that I would help you transition into *one of them!*" she said the last word in a scowl.

Kaiden knew what he was suggesting. *I'm a monster. An abomination. A liability to the cause.*

Kaiden Ottaker was a hybrid, an abomination to the two species of Elders and Shifters that lived on the planet, locked in an eternal war. He was born to Shifter parents, but after they had been killed by the Elders, the Shifter scientist, Professor Williams, took him in – and had a plan.

No Shifter could get near the Elders, not unless they caught them in the rare times that they travelled between the cities, and usually then the Elders travelled in armoured trains with hundreds of mortal servitor guards. The Shifters had to fight their wars either through human sympathisers – the insurgents – or had to try to infiltrate the alien urban environment to get to their natural enemies.

The Shifters could barely control their rage as it was. Any alliance of packs and tribes against the Elders lasted a brief, blood-filled summer before the tribes broke apart under their own internecine rivalries. At the moment, Alpha Lubok was the strongest Shifter and pack-leader on the East Coast, but ever since that fateful day when Professor William's 'pet project' had gone wrong, Lubok hadn't managed to command enough forces to fight back against the Elders in the cities.

And all because of Kaiden.

The young man remembered the day that the Professor, his mentor, had explained the idea to him. "No Shifter can move as fast as an Elder, and no non-Elder will pass the scans that lead into the Elder sanctuaries. We need an Elder to work *for* us, or make one."

What? his younger self had said.

Professor Williams, with his big, nervous smile had explained, "You have the opportunity to do something truly incredible. To fight back against the Elders who killed your parents. Once and for all. We know that the Elders are a symbiotic species, just as the Shifters are. The Elders have a blood-virus that melds with the mortal DNA and RNA. Before, the two species were incompatible, but I think that I have found a way to synthesize them. A Blood Doll slowly becomes more of a host for the virus until becoming a Servitor – still technically a human, but half vampire. With the right process, the virus takes over completely and they become a fully-blooded Elder. I can do that to you!"

Kaiden, still young and full of rage about his parents, had agreed to the transition. He'd had no idea of the months of agonizing blood transfusions and the changes that would occur inside him. The rage. The anger.

The problem was that no one had thought that I could Shift too, Kaiden thought grimly. He had never shown an aptitude for it. The Shifter-virus in his veins had made him tougher, with sharper senses, but he had shown no propensity to take on any other animal's shape, ever.

It was the Elder virus that had brought that on, and made him the Beast of New York.

"There's a girl," Kaiden said. "An Elder."

"What have you done Kaiden?" the Guide sister started to snarl.

"She was being attacked by Blood Dolls, or who appeared to be Blood Dolls," Kaiden answered.

"Lubock's blood traps," The Guide sister nodded. "You know the plan. Entice the unwary Elders, and then, when you get a chance, disable them or bring them in for testing. He wasn't to find out what they know."

"He has something, some new kind of drug. It almost killed her," Kaiden said. He didn't want to tell the Guide sister how, seeing the woman being treated like that, as an experiment, as just another plaything in a greater war had made him mad.

"So?" the Guide sister said. "Lubok is going to know it was you, unless you killed the witnesses." The Guide sister had no great love for the Shifter pack-commander, thinking him a brute and a fool, but that did not mean that she would ever help his enemies.

"I know. But I think this Elder is different. She seemed young, a Feral maybe. As she was recovering, she talked in her sleep about sunshine, fields. She remembers being mortal."

"So? I remember being a child – but it doesn't mean I want to go back!" The Guide sister started shaking her head.

"Please, sister. I think she can help us. Professor Williams' plan, it was a good one. If I can convince her that she can trust me, trust us..." Kaiden pleaded, trying to stop himself from ripping the bag of blood in half and drinking it then and there.

"Trust *us*? There is no *us*, Kaiden. You are an outcast to the Shifters, and the Elders want to kill us all. It's just you, and foolish me who's taken pity on you because we once knew the Professor!" The Guide sister was pacing back and forth.

"Then I'll do it myself," Kaiden said finally. "The Professor had a good plan, and I'm not about to let him down."

The Guide sister, herself a human mortal, whose family must have a Shifter in its ancestry somewhere, sniffed the air. The Shifters always said that they could sense honesty and lies.

"Okay." She snatched two more bags of plasma and blood, putting them into Kaiden's shaking hands. "Here. This will have to do, but heaven help me. You know that this pet Elder of yours will want feeding, and she will want to dream. What will you do when she starts going out to feed on innocent mortals?"

"I'll stop her. I'll take her to the Blood Banks..." Kaiden was looking at all of the blood in his hands, trying to convince himself that he wasn't excited.

"You'll get yourself caught, you mean. No, you come back here. Bring her. We'll see whether we really can trust this Feral of yours. Now, we've spent too much time already." The Guide sister snapped the case shut, drawing the curtains back down again. Without even waiting to see whether Kaiden was going or staying, she pushed her way through to the markets beyond. Kaiden heard the jangle of her bells get fainter and fainter, before it was finally swallowed by the noise of the market around them.

Kaiden wasn't even in sight of the end of the market when he heard the commotion behind him. It was the sound of running feet getting closer. He tensed his shoulders, the superior senses that he had inherited from his Shifter parents informing him of the wave of adrenaline and sweat that infused the narrow alleyway suddenly, as the other traders expected the worst.

"Hey! You!" The running stopped behind him. There was no way for him to disguise the fact that they were shouting *at* him – but he did anyway. He kept walking, trudging forward, calculating the distance.

"I said stop. *Abomination.*" The title was flung at him like an insult, and, at that point, Kaiden knew that it was over. He couldn't run. He would have to turn and face them.

On either side of him, as he slowly turned to face his pursuers, he saw the nearest stall-holders quickly starting to pull down blinds, or gather up their most expensive items from the front of their small wooden tables. It was the look on their faces that made Kaiden wonder. They were worried, but not fearful for their lives.

It's not the servitors then, not the servants of the Elders, Kaiden knew.

No, who he saw in front of him were not the white-suited human enforcers, all blood-bound to their Elder masters. Instead, he saw three figures approaching him in that wary walk that attackers always had before a fight. They looked like drifters, the first in ragged leather and denim clothes, a bandana holding back partially dyed hair, his leather jaggedly ripped off at the sleeves and showing bare knees. The second was a little thinner, with a Mohawk, and the third was a woman with braids, slowly putting a duffel bag on the ground.

Shifters, Kaiden thought.

"Now, I don't want any trouble..." he growled, nodding to the edge of the market where, for certain, there would be some Servitors stationed and waiting to pounce on anything that even dared to look suspicious.

The first, Bandana, Kaiden thought, sneered. "Trouble?" he said, his voice thick. "You were trouble on the day you were *made*, mate." His voice was guttural and harsh, like a dog's.

"I wasn't made. I was born," Kaiden bristled. He knew exactly what they were insinuating. That he was like one of *them*, an Elder. He could feel the headache starting behind his eyes, a sign that his pupils were dilating, that he was ready to change.

I can't do it here. I can't allow myself to change in front of anyone here. Kaiden could feel the weight of the blood bags pressing against his chest under his coat. He had to keep them safe as well, for the Feral's sake.

The thought of all of that blood, so close to him, only made him all the more angry. *Or was it hungry?* He tried not to think to himself.

"Well. I know who you are. I know *what* you are." Bandana was jeering at him, striding closer, oddly confident given the rumour that Kaiden was supposed to be some kind of monster.

"I'm warning you. Stay away from me…" Kaiden was thinking about the blood under his vest, how close it was, how long it had been since he had dreamed…

Bandana laughed, casually taking out from his waistband a pistol the size of his head. "How about you come with me? I'm sure that Lubok will just *love* to see what you've been up to…" Bandana turned around to laugh with his friends. It was his first mistake.

Kaiden grabbed the pistol with one hand, forcing it away from him. It went off with a deafening roar, but already Kaiden was moving in, reaching for the man's throat with his outstretched fingers. He was already looking at the other two on the other side of him, seeing their faces turn to alarm, and then to anger as a physical shiver started to overtake them.

They're changing, Kaiden thought, his hand closing on Bandana's windpipe. Before he even knew what he was doing, he had already lifted him off of the ground, raising him into the air so his feet dangled over the pavement. Somewhere there was a scream, and something brushed past his shoulder.

Mohawk and Braids were twitching now, their limbs spasming as they coughed and their eyes rolled, their mouths frothing with spittle. Kaiden knew he had mere microseconds to act. The virus that infected the Shifters was different from the Elders'. It was much more aggressive in scope and effect. Like many other viruses, it infected the DNA and RNA of the host, and carried with it the coding of previous dominant species that it had infected. Over the centuries, there were 'wolvish' strains of the Shifter virus, as well as 'feline' and 'bear'.

Kaiden was somewhat lucky – these Shifters appeared to be one of the only Shifter communities that actually *liked* to spend times in the cities.

Rat-shifters.

The pain scored him again, this time not on his shoulder, but the arm that was busy choking Bandana. Mohawk, who was now taller, with the head of a malformed rat, and whose human clothes sat awkwardly in a body that rippled with muscles and fur – drew his hand back to use the chain-whip again against Kaiden.

There. The smell engulfed Kaiden's nostrils. *Blood.* A mixture of his own from the tiny lacerations from the whip, and that of Bandana whose neck was slowly being crushed.

Kaiden felt a flicker of anger from deep within him, hunger – and the whole world flashed bright and dark.

The next swing from the chain-whip by Mohawk met Kaiden's new form across the shoulders. He grabbed the line and yanked, dragging Mohawk towards him as he threw the mess that was Bandana onto the wooden stalls and cheap goods.

Kaiden didn't have time to think about Braids, because already Mohawk had latched his long snout around his arm, incisors piercing his muscles.

Kaiden roared, and his rage sounded alien to his ears. Inhuman screeching, a cross between a chitter and a wolfish snarl. More blood was spilling everywhere, and Mohawk was latched onto his chest, biting him again and again.

Kaiden used his greater strength to pry Mohawk's jaw from his shoulders, leaving an exposed neck. He bit down, deep. The taste of hot iron, warm and sticky. His teeth like a dog's canines tearing.

For a moment there was nothing. Sunlight in the trees. Birdcall, and warmth on Kaiden's face. He felt at peace.

Safe.

Kaiden opened his eyes to screaming and the sound of alarms. One of the stallholders was lying on her back, blood spattered over her, screaming and pointing. There were high-pitched alarms that hurt his ears, whistle-like peeps and shrieks.

The Servitors! Kaiden had cause to recall that whistle. He knew that was the sound of their imminent arrival.

"Get up, beast!" someone was hissing, and he turned around to see the silver-haired old woman behind him, prodding his back with her staff.

"I'm not a beast!" he slurred, before he realized what he was holding in his hands: A human head, which was still sporting a Mohawk. Shifters transform back into their natural biological shape once they die.

Looking around him, Kaiden could see that it looked as though a bomb had gone off in the small alleyway. The stalls nearest were all destroyed, a pile of wooden staves and torn canvas. Fruit and clothes were trampled into the dirt, and the scene was awash with blood and unidentifiable bits of flesh. Kaiden remembered the fight, and he winced as the wounds on his arms and shoulders suddenly made themselves known.

"Oh no," Kaiden said, looking at his hands. They were red with blood.

PHEEP! PHWEEP! The whistled alarms sounded again, getting closer. Kaiden looked up, thinking that he could see the flash of a white helmet in the distance, past the lines of scarves and awnings. It was the Servitors, and when they arrived they wouldn't just bring reinforcements, they would bring guns too; lots of guns, and a live video-feed back to whatever sanctuary of Elders was currently monitoring the sunlit mortal city.

And then his secret would be out. They would capture him and find out just what he was: An almost-Elder and almost-Shifter.

"Yes! That's right! It's them – and when they get here they'll throw you in a test tube and cut you up until even you won't be able to recover from it!" the Guide Sister was saying. "Here." She handed him a rucksack, half unzipped, which was stuffed full of blood bags. "You might as well take this – when they get here they'll search the whole market anyway, and they'll throw me in with you if they find it. You might as well take it, as you need it!" She thrust it at him, turning and starting to hobble off quickly into the depths of the market.

"Oh." Kaiden looked at the bag. Blood. Lots of it, and all of it contraband. He suddenly realised that his mouth and the lower half of his jaw must be soaked in the stuff; he remembered as through a bad dream biting down on gristle and muscle. Kaiden's dreams were dark, and thick, and when he looked at the rucksack full of food, he did not feel hungry. He must have had his fill, and transformed back into his normal mortal frame while he was recovering.

Oh no. They saw me. The stall-holders... Kaiden got unsteadily to his feet, looking for an exit.

PHEEP! PHWEEP! The whistles were almost on top of him, and he finally managed to shake a bit of sense into his brain. He took off at a run, upsetting carts and stalls as he did so.

4. The Decisions of an Archon

"The Seventh Rule of the Predatory Society: Blood, like Power, must be contained."

- The Rule of Archons, Seventh Mandate.

Jeremiah was woken from his slumber by the uncomfortable pulse of a blue-filter light into his crypt. It was one of the few concessions to modernity that the Archon of Brooklyn had agreed on installing in his inner sanctum, even though it ruined his image of an ancient methuselah.

The pulse of blue-filter light was as near to the UV range so as to be uncomfortable and mildly irritating, but not enough to actually burn the skin of an Elder. The vampires used this technology often to annoy, disrupt, or even torture fellow Elders when they had to.

For Jeremiah, it meant that he was woken at a time when he should be in the deep, dreamless, coma-like sleep that all of the fully-blooded Elders sank into during the hours of daylight. He snarled, his forward canines sliding into place as he reached up and clicked off the waking-pulse from the dark space where he slept. A few seconds later and the hatch of the metal cylinder slid away, and he was leaning forward, and stepping out. Already a Servitor, with her shaved bald head and white clothes, was stepping forward to brush the dust from his back, which he lined his crypt with.

It was a ridiculous affectation, of course, but some vampiric scholars believed that the grave soil acted as a culture for the virus that swam in their veins, and Archon Jeremiah was eager to follow tradition.

He was the youngest Archon – and that meant that the other Archons of the City of New York tended to ignore him. He did not remember the founding of America, the fall of the Bastille, or the brilliance of Galileo Galilei.

Not that all of them remember it either! Jeremiah was in a bad mood, as vampires awakened in the daytime were wont to be. *Half of their brains have turned to mush, and they are but fit to be corpse food!* He scoffed as he jabbed at his personal Servitor to leave him now. Whilst Archon Jeremiah was envious of his older brethren, he was also fully aware that the virus that gave him life would also, one day, turn him into a creature beyond reckoning – and beyond mortality. In the end, the oldest of the vampires become little more that walking husks of dried skin, bones, and claws.

"What is it? Why have I been awakened?" he said loudly, and the shaved-headed woman said in a meek voice,

"There has been a disturbance, sir, in the mortal marketplace." She bowed her head and kept it looking at his finely-tailored shoes of red Spanish leather.

"What of it? Isn't there always – I was disturbed for this!?" Jeremiah was fully ready to tear the woman's head off and demand a report from the Day Shift Security Counsel, when the woman said fearfully at his side,

"Shifter presence has been confirmed, sire."

Jeremiah hissed. *Shifters. In the city again. Did no one ever patrol the streets during the day?* He set off at a quick pace through the low-light chambers of his sanctum, far under the city.

The lair of an Archon was always a lavish affair, although different Archons chose to display their status in different ways. Jeremiah did so with polished, wood-panelled walls, and iron doors engraved with heraldic devices from vampiric history. He stalked past dragons and bats, strange winged cats, and more nefarious monsters.

A part of his status entailed keeping an active administration running at all times – which could be troublesome for a being that spends half of the day in a torpor. Instead, the Archons employed small armies of their blood-bound human Servitors; usually ex-Blood Dolls or those mortals who had been picked out of the human security industry and force-fed Elder blood until they started to take on some of the virus to become half-Elder.

These mortal Servitors could work and walk unimpeded through the daylight (although they felt a vague sense of discomfort, such as having a mild hangover). However, the benefit of their strength, speed, and reactions was incredible. It was these white-garbed Servitors who manned the 'Solar Stability' factories, and Servitors who patrolled the streets on behalf of their slumbering masters.

He stormed into the Day Shift Security office, throwing open the iron double doors to reveal a command room with overhead displays, flat screens, and rows upon rows of white-garbed workers. Their fingers clattered away at their desks, and, overhead, Jeremiah saw the screens shift from one street to another, an aerial view of one block, a close-up of a group of Servitors conducting a house-to-house search.

"What is it? Why have I been awakened?" he barked, waiting for Matthias, one of his oldest Servitors, who stood up quickly. The white of his encounter suit contrasted with his black skin.

"Shifters, sire, a fight in the human markets: Rodenti-sapiens," he used their full description, and clicked a remote control at the largest of the overhead screens.

They flickered to an aerial view of the river, before zooming in towards a darker smear across the cityscape, caught between the water and the ordered blocks of the urban landscape beyond. It always seemed to Jeremiah that the markets were spreading every year, stretching out past their ruined wasteland re-development to encroach more upon the city.

Jeremiah felt his lips curling, and his forward incisors starting to slip forward. He felt hot and angry just at seeing this extravagant display of mortal rebellion.

The view started to zoom in, closer and closer, and the Archon realized that they must be following the recording of one of the patrol drones that the Elders widely used now to patrol the wakeful city.

"The Eye was activated automatically when a gunshot was heard coming from the market, quite a way in," Mathias said by means of explanation.

"Gunshot?" Jeremiah felt guardedly impressed. If the Shifters had managed to smuggle guns into his Brooklyn, then they really *were* planning something. "But none of ours were hurt?" he asked.

"No, sire. No Servitors, none of the Blood-Bound. But the results were... *interesting*." Matthias flicked the control to speed up the flight of the drone 'Eye'. It flashed over buildings and past windows, before dropping lower and flying at speeds towards a dark, sheltered part of the market.

From this high up, it was clear to see that some sort of commotion had taken place. The usually-ramshackle lines of stalls and alleyways were even more broken up in one place, and it was obvious that a number of stalls had been torn apart. At the periphery of the drone's vision, there could be seen the retreating scurries of stall-holders as they fled the fight or the justice that was about to visit them.

"The local patrol was alerted and dispatched at the same time of course, but the Eye got there first," Matthias continued.

The Eye stopped moving, hovering in place to try to record what had happened, and Jeremiah saw a few jerky frames of a man having a rushed conversation with an older, white-haired woman, before they both fled.

The Eye remained on the scene as the Servitors arrived, taking more shots of the aftermath and the evidence that they had found. Blood everywhere, splashed all over the broken marketplace.

Jeremiah felt a sharp pang of hunger lance up through his chest. The mere sight of the red stuff made his pulse start to beat. "Who was he? What am I watching? Some Shifter quarrel?"

The Archon thought that it was just as well if the savage brutes had decided to start fighting each other. It did, after all, make his job a lot easier.

"We thought so at first, sire, which is why the Eye remained with the patrol. But then..." Matthias clicked away from the screen, and the view of the white-suited patrol Servitors were replaced by green graphs and chemical analysis charts. Numbers and data swam into view.

Jeremiah wasn't very good at the sciences, preferring the traditional vampiric interests of the arts, but over the last a hundred years he had picked up a passing familiarity with them.

"That is the Shifter virus," he said, and Matthias nodded, enhancing one part of the data set to show a collection of green morphing and moving cells. They had strange hooks that pushed out from their green cell-walls, expanding the cell and distorting it to try and take on odd shapes; vaguely octagonal, fuzzily rectangular, before reverting to rounded again.

"Yes, sire, this is the Shifter virus recovered from the, uh, the blood at the scene. As you see, it is trying to replicate and transform into remembered cell configurations to heal its host," Matthias explained. "Obviously, it cannot do that as the host is in a hundred pieces and on the ground, but the Shifter virus is nothing if not persistent." Matthias next showed a scan from the Blood Banks. "Our records don't match precisely, so these Shifters must have come from outside of the city, although their DNA blood-grouping does give a strong affinity for the coastal mortal families, and the East Coast in general."

"And that..." Jeremiah felt even his cold flesh pale when he saw the next data-set come into view.

There was the green Shifter-virus, this time much less aggressive and less advanced than the others, with the spikes trying to morph the cell body only in smaller, softer ways. However, there was something else very peculiar about these cells. They had within them another colour: the reddish colour of the vampiric Lych-virus.

"Yes, sire, it is," Matthias said heavily. "This was recovered from the scene, although the traces were small. It was a stroke of luck that the analysers picked it up."

The vampiric Lych-virus was unmistakeable. It appeared to look a little like the bio-hazard symbol that the mortals sometimes used, a collection of red tentacles spearing out of a small host nuclei. It used these sharp 'pincers' to seize other cells and pierce them, sucking their nutrients and re-encoding them with their own reddened Lych-structure.

The red, piercing tentacles were extending outwards from the greenish blob of a Shifter cell, and the Archon watched as they acted symbiotically to try to morph and grow, expand and contract.

"Is that what I think it is?" Jeremiah's voice was deadly cold.

"Yes, sire. It is stable. A fusion of Shifter and Lych virus." Matthias nodded.

"And we have samples?" Jeremiah raised one finely-sculpted eyebrow.

"As much as we could gather," Matthias said again, his voice monotoned. The discovery was momentous, but it was so large that no one in the room could even think around the magnitude of it. For decades they had been attempting to modify the Shifter virus – to get it to self-destruct or to find a way for the Lych-virus to defeat it. Every attempt at marrying the two had been a failure.

Until now.

"And we have footage of the two...*survivors?*" Jeremiah said carefully.

Matthias nodded.

"Then come with me, Matthias." He nodded, leading his trusted servant out of the double doors, and closing them behind him.

Everyone in that room had seen it. They all knew that it existed, Jeremiah was thinking as he, very purposefully, keyed in the code to lock the door silently behind him.

"Sire?" Matthias' voice rose just a little, a touch of alarm.

"It is fine, Matthias, it is fine," Jeremiah soothed him. "Now, I am going to tell you to aid me in a very simple set of tasks, which will require absolute discretion, of course."

"As always, I am your servant in all things," Matthias bowed his head and said instantly.

"Good. Then we will begin..." Jeremiah took a step towards his Servitor, and lowered his voice so, even in the deserted corridor, only the man could barely hear his commands. At first Matthias's eyes flared wide as he realized what his Archon was saying, but then he nodded, too terrified or indoctrinated to do anything but agree.

"Of course, sire. Immediately. As you wish." The Servitor stepped back after he had finished, threw a sharp salute, before turning and running down the corridor quickly.

The aerial Eye drones were not the only drones that the Elders used throughout their cities. There were some as big as small dogs, others as big as cars and like small planes – only without the pilots, crew, or passengers. They usually carried a much deadlier cargo, and it was these heavier aerial drones that woke up remotely from their rooftop hangers, sliding out into the weak sunshine like robotic birds of prey.

With a hum and a whirr of systems waking up, they flew into the air above Brooklyn.

For a symbiotic species as ancient as the vampires, that could theoretically live for thousands of years each, they were also surprisingly technological. The vampires had seen the power of industry and technology rise from its very earliest inception to the modern day. They had seen how fast technology had changed their lives and all of those who used it. The world had shrunk over a course of decades, not centuries. The vampires had decided to seize the technology whenever they could, commanding it to enslave the mortal day-struck humans.

The Reaper drones fell toward the edge of the river, speeding low over the rooftops and past windows as they neared their target: The mortal marketplace. With a sound like breaking thunder, rockets fell from their metal bellies to arc, as quick as lightning, through the sky to the spot where the fight between Kaiden, Bandana, Mohawk, and Braids had so recently taken place.

The ground trembled as they found their target, sending clouds of black smoke and fire hundreds of feet into the sky. All traces of the fight, and the Lych-Shifter virus, were eradicated.

And a good percentage of any potential witnesses, too.

For the not-entirely mortal witnesses to this scene, they met a different fate. Just before the white-clothed Servitors heard the red warning signs of the dispatched Reapers across the city, their door was unlocked (none of them had even noticed that the door had been locked, as it was still the middle of their shift). In walked ten angry and awakened Elders from the Archon's own brood, woken by Matthias himself from their crypts, and with Jeremiah at their head.

They closed the door behind them, and then the screams began.

Jeremiah knew that he would have many questions to face from the other Archons of the city, but he also knew that he had in his command the only viable sample of a Lych-Shifter mutation – and Archon Jeremiah was not a vampire to share his toys willingly.

5. Tay, Waking Up

"The time of Friendship is over; the time of Family has ended, you now have a new pact; a covenant that is stronger than those mortal ties. No more will frailty, weakness, or death diminish you. You are remade, and all mortal and weak bonds are broken."

- The Litany of the Elders; On Transformation.

When Tay next awoke, the night was just starting to rise. The murky colour of daylight was being replaced by the pinks and gloomy purples of sunset, before mixing with the yellowish glare of the streetlights outside. In a city as big as New York, quite often the night-time didn't really herald darkness, just a different type of light.

She yawned and rolled over, expecting to see her crypt in her tiny, shabby apartment. Instead, her eyes were greeted by the sight of stained oil canvases, discarded boxes.

Oh yeah, she thought, remembering giddily what had happened over the last twenty-four hours. *I've been ill. The drug. The fight, and someone saving me. Feral.*

She remembered the word more than the slap from Jeremiah, and somehow the word made her even angrier. *Now that I have no home in the city, I'll starve...* She realized, before her mind caught up to the fact that she wasn't actually hungry, not at all.

In fact, I feel pretty full, she marvelled, luxuriating in the sense of strength from her muscles, and relaxedness of her mind. Dreaming always gave her a sense of peace, but she couldn't remember when she had...

"I fed you," a voice said from the corner of the room, and Tay sprang, cat-like, to her haunches. It was the man. The one who had saved her. He was sitting by the table, wrapping a bandage around his forearm where it seemed like an ugly-looking wound had recently been inflicted there. On the table was a mess of firearms, ammo clips, and bullets.

Does he mean to kill me? The girl looked at the small armoury on the table. *No, he saved my life. What does he want?*

"You... *fed* me?" she said slowly, looking at the man's wounds.

He gave her a crooked smile. "No, it wasn't mine. You'd know if it was my blood. This was someone else trying to bite me," he sighed heavily.

"Do you get bitten a lot?" Tay found herself asking, easing into a standing position. "You don't seem the usual type..."

"What, a Blood Brother? No. I can't stand them myself," Kaiden said. "Kaiden. We met last night."

"I remember." Tay didn't move to shake his hand.

"I'm surprised. Lubok's new drug knocked you out pretty good." Kaiden finished his bandage and tied it off.

"Lubok?" *The name meant something...* Tay was sure that she had heard it before, maybe at one of those dreary security meetings that Jeremiah held for his brood.

"He's the Alpha around here. Tribal leader of a whole number of packs for the East Coast. Mean as hell, and ugly to go with it," Kaiden smirked.

Shifter, Tay remembered in an instant, feeling herself tense up and her forward incisors slide out in a cat-like snarl. *Lubok was the name of some big Shifter that Jeremiah was always worried about. It all makes sense.* She looked at the piles of guns and ammo, the rugged, faintly survivalist air that this 'Kaiden' had. Living like a drifter, a vigilante in the city, and he knew how to fight...

"It's not what you think," the man said, but Tay was already moving. She reached the door of his apartment and stopped, slowed by the fact that the man hadn't stood up to halt her, or even say anything. He just remained seated, looking at her with that crooked smirk on his face.

Tay halted by the door, her hand on the lock. "You're not going to stop me? I'm not captured?"

"You're free to go anytime – although right now might not be such a great idea. A large section of downtown is a smoking pile of rubble." Kaiden flicked his hand to the table and from somewhere there clicked on a small, crackling radio. They didn't have to wait long before the news came around again.

"Scenes of confusion earlier today as some sort of security action was taken in the Brooklyn river markets, killing eighty souls, and even one team of Servitors. Archon Jeremiah – hail to his name – is reported as saying that an incursion of Shifter insurgents in the city had been stopped at only the last possible moment by decisive action taken from the Day Shift staff..."

"Live from the sight, our reporter, Chandauri Rajavan, describes the devastation visible..."

Kaiden clicked it off. "The streets are flooded with Servitors. I wouldn't be out there alone if I were you." His eyes flickered. "If I were a Feral."

"Who says that I am-?" Tay began, but her words sounded stupid even to her. It was obvious that no Elder already welcomed into a brood would be the prey of random Blood Dolls on the street, or wandering half-starved in the alleyways of Brooklyn anyway. "Okay," she murmured, walking back into the room (but making sure that she never turned her back on him), and crouching down once more by the mattress where she had so recently crouched. Tay looked at the man's bandaged arms once more.

"So... I didn't feed off you – then who was it?" she asked, a little nervously. The thought of feeding without even having a connection to the person or place was unsettling, like waking up in a stranger's bed without any recollection of how she had gotten there.

Oh yeah. Tick, just done that, Tay thought.

"These." Kaiden kicked the bag underneath the table, which spilled open to reveal a dozen or so fresh bags of blood. "I'm rotating them in and out of the freezer. We've got enough to last us a month or so."

We…? Tay registered, but didn't ask. *Was he a Servitor then? An Elder?* The vampire opened her mouth and gently tasted the air, allowing the chemical chromosomes to register against her heightened taste buds. *No. Definitely not.* But there was something there that she couldn't quite place. It wasn't the same earth-like taste that mortal humans exuded, and neither was it the sort of instant-recognition that she had from other Elders. Something else.

Something new.

"So, why am I here? How do you know…*Lubok?*" Tay looked around, from the guns to the blood, and back to the man again.

"He and I are, uh, you could say old acquaintances," Kaiden said easily. He didn't appear worried that he was suggesting to an Elder that he was in league with the insurgents.

He must know how bad it is for the Ferals. No Elder would listen to me if I turned up at a sanctuary, would they? But with a piece of information like this, however… Tay thought, and instantly her stomach turned at the thought of giving someone up who had just possibly saved her un-life.

But he is an insurgent – he pretty much said as much! Tay argued with herself as the strange man continued.

"More enemies, maybe. Lubok has some new drug that he's dosing his own Blood Dolls and Brothers with, sending them out to bring in as many Elders as possible. He's fighting a war, you see, and he'll stop at nothing to win it."

"Well, if the radio is right, then it looks as though he has already lost pretty spectacularly," Tay said, feeling a little more at ease than before. She didn't know what it was about this man – but he wasn't giving off the usual signals that an attacker would. If anything, he just looked tired.

"No. The market attack was Elder retaliation for... *something else*." The man examined his array of guns intently for a second, before his voice came back, softer than before. "Let me be straight with you, Feral. I *need* you, and I think that you need me."

Tay pursed her lips. "Tell me more."

"I know Lubok, and, even though his goal is true, he is a cruel son-of-a..." the man's voice petered off as he stared off into the middle distance, remembering something far away. "And you... Well, you need a steady access to blood, and safety. You have no crypt, no sanctuary, no brood. It will only be a matter of time before the mortals and the Shifters break under the strain of the Elders, and there will be blood on the streets."

"There has always been blood on the streets," Tay said, stepping quietly around the man to the blinded window, opening two to look below. They were about ten stories up. Below them, neon streetlights fizzled in the dreary, constant rain that the solar programme seemed to inspire. "I know our histories. Civil wars, uprisings, revolutions." She was tired of reciting the litany of despair that was now her blood-right. "And it always ends the same way. Always us Elders on top." She turned around to him, seeing him gaze at the table. "We have the advantage of time, you see. The Archon-system means that they can plan in decades, a few rulers setting in plan events generations into the future. Who knows what they have planned for the city by the time I am old and you are dead?"

"It's different this time." Kaiden looked up suddenly.

"How?" Tay thought he was being overdramatic. She maintained a superior air, condescending, slipping into the speech patterns that the Elders always used for mortals.

"You felt the drug. Just a normal feed and you were as weak as a baby, for two mortals to do whatever they wanted with you.

That is what Lubok has in mind for you all. Slaughter," Kaiden growled.

Tay *did* remember the drug, the awful, cloying heaviness of it as it had sat on her mind, robbing her muscles of their coordination and strength.

"Well. All it takes is for Lubok to get the drug into the Blood Banks, and all of a sudden every visiting Servitor or Elder in the city is paralysed. You were a test, and it worked," Kaiden said.

The vampire didn't want to agree to it, but it was true. A blood-borne drug wouldn't take long to pass through the entire system. There was one thing that she didn't understand though. "What about you, though? Why do you care, if you are on the side of the insurgents?"

Only now did Kaiden stand up and walk towards Tay. The girl tensed, expecting him to attack, but he merely reached past her to twitch the metal blinds open still further. As he stood there, her heightened senses could pick up the strong scent of maleness coming off of him: A hint of wood, smoke, and sweat.

"There." He was nodding to an area downtown where the neon lights were shaded and reflected on an ugly haze of post-destruction smoke. The pall from the missiles used was still rising, and filling the sky. "You know as well as I do that it will be the mortals who get stuck in the middle of all of this. It is those who are the most defenceless who will be targeted, persecuted. The Elders will search for anyone they can call an insurgent, and burn down whole neighbourhoods, and the Shifters will not stop in their search for vengeance. It doesn't matter if you are a misguided, mortal Blood Doll, or a brain-washed Servitor. Hundreds, thousands will die before it is over – and the city will be destroyed."

Tay stared out at the rising smoke, thinking for a long time. Of course, Kaiden was right. It *was* the mortals who would suffer the worst, and she had already decided long ago not to participate in the culls that Archon Jeremiah had ordered for her sector.

When she was younger, it had all seemed so simple. She had thought of the Elders as glamorous and darkly beautiful. They were almost gods that existed above them all, floating like ethereal stars above the constellation of society. Cold, and cruel.

When Tay was older, however (in years, if not in physical appearance), she had seen that the Elders that she had joined were not god-like celebrities. They were, if anything, *less* than the life she had come from before. They existed in a strange, self-supporting, self-reverential world, uncaring of whatever became of the mortals underneath them.

Maybe it was because Tay was still a young Elder, but she could not live like that. Maybe she still remembered her lost humanity all too keenly when she *dreamed*. For a terrible moment, Tay wondered, *Am I just going to become like the rest of my kind when I get older? Will I, too, cease to care about the always-changing faces of the mortals underneath me? Their lives that flicker in and out so easily?*

Right now, Tay thought of the Elders as more of a sort of biological shepherding system (which was, of course, what the Elder's propaganda promoted). The Elders had to live *off* of their mortals, but that didn't mean that they had to be tyrants. In this day and age, there were plenty of opportunities for non-harmful blood donations and blood banks. Whole industries had been set up to ensure the speed and comfort of the whole process, to reduce concern and antagonism on the part of the mortals.

To reduce waste, she thought rather more cynically.

"Okay," Tay said carefully. "What do you propose?" She turned to Kaiden.

"I want to stop Lubok's plan, but that doesn't mean I want life to go back to being ruled by the Archons. The Archons are evil too," Kaiden growled, and Tay felt a shiver of something primal at the deep, guttural promise in the man's throat.

"I don't see how you can have both..." Tay began to say.

"We have to find a way. To stop the Archons *and* Lubok," Kaiden insisted.

"But-" Tay protested.

"We *have* to, if we want to save this city." Kaiden looked out over the cityscape. "If we want to save them."

The woman was silent for a long while, looking at the neon lights, the moving glare of street traffic, the distant sound of shouting, music, and people going about their daily business. She remembered a time when it wasn't always like this, when she had the sun on her closed eyes and her hands ran over the green fronds of fresh sweetcorn sheaths...

"Yes. I'll do it. I'll help you," she said, just as there was a loud scream from outside Kaiden's apartment.

6. The Duties of Pack & Brood

"Follow your Alpha, listen to your Beta, look after your Omega. That is the rule of the Pack."

- Three-Feathers Law of the Pack (Shifter Oral Histories)

When the scream shattered the usual silence of Kaiden's hideout, Tay felt a cold certainty in her belly, one that she couldn't quite ignore.

"Uh... Is that normal for around here?" she asked Kaiden, and from the look of the way that he was frantically picking up heavy Glocks and ammo-clips, it certainly wasn't.

"It might just be that asshat junkie from downstairs..." Kaiden was already shrugging on his coat, and stuffing blood packs into a rucksack. "We're going to need this."

He said 'we're' again... Tay thought quickly. *As if he needs the blood...*

"I know a place," Tay said, in a rush.

"Huh?" Kaiden kept his voice low as he glowered at her.

Why isn't his glower threatening to me? Tay thought. *This man could kill me with this much weaponry and all I can think is that he just looks cute!*

"Don't worry," the vampire said, heading in the opposite direction, towards the window. "Jackson is a friend; he owns a bar in Manhattan, and he's someone who doesn't like our Archon, Jeremiah, too much anyway." Tay almost laughed to herself. In her experience, no one actually did like Jeremiah at all, but Jackson, being under the auspices of a different Archon of the city, didn't actually have to click his heels and jump to attention if Jeremiah ordered.

Jackson might trust us. She nodded to herself. *He might do. He has to.*

"That might be too risky..." Kaiden was saying, but his words were cut off by the sudden farting *brrp* of a semi-automatic machine gun. A bulky, small sort, messy in close quarters.

"I think sticking around *here* is going to be riskier still," Tay remarked. "I take it that you can climb?"

"There's a metal staircase out there, but wait – dammit..." Kaiden's hand was on the door when he heard it. The howl.

The sound ululated from below, probably near the ground floor, and it was followed by sharp, barking laughter.

"Shifters!" Tay snarled, forward incisors lengthening and her hands starting to curl into claws. She had been taught that Shifters would mean only one thing – blood and death. "These your friends, are they?" she snarled, tearing back the metal blinds to be suddenly flooded in neon streetlight. Tay kicked savagely at the window, causing it to smash and let in the cold, drizzly night air beyond.

"No – don't!" Kaiden was shouting, turning to watch her just as the howling-voice rose up again, echoing across the hallway.

"KAAAAY-DEN! COME OUT NOW, COME OUT! WE HEAR YOU'VE GOT A FERAL PRESENT FOR US!!"

Kaiden, one hand on the door and the other on the gun, looked in horror towards Tay, starting to shake his head. "The Guide sister, they must have... She must have..."

Tay felt almost incandescent with rage. "I knew this was too good to be true. What was all that about you and me saving the city together? You appealing to my better nature? Huh?" She felt a fool, she felt used. *Just like Jeremiah always did.*

It would serve him right, leaving him here, Tay thought for a second as she watched her saviour. *This was probably his plan all along – to wait for his pals and Shifter allies to turn up and tear me limb from limb. The whole thing was all a ploy!*

The vampire saw it all too clearly now. It must have been a trap. She felt hurt, betrayed, and, although she didn't have any connection to the man, she felt like he had just kicked her in the gut.

Well. I don't need rescuing. I don't need anyone, Tay thought angrily, turning and climbing as quickly as a cat out onto the ledge beyond.

"No! Wait!" the man called Kaiden was saying, and she heard him running to the open window behind her as more shouts could clearly be heard deeper inside the building, running towards them.

Cold air surrounded Tay as she scampered along the ledge, using her new-found vitality and superior reflexes to scramble on feet and hands to the corner of the building, which was ten feet above a streetlight. Behind her, she heard a sound like a loud bang, and then snarls, and the farting report of gun fire.

I can't wait, she thought, hurling herself down to catch the streetlight with her hands, using it to swing herself across to the next light, and then onto the side of a balcony on the other side of the street. For a moment, everything was whirling bright and dark patches, adrenaline flooding her system, the ragged burn of air in her lungs. The whole movement took her only a matter of seconds as her super-fast reflexes kicked in.

Just a couple of stories from the street level now, she flipped herself over the balcony edge as lights came in on the building inside, and then loud, angry shouts from high above her.

She swung, dropping herself onto the roof of a parked truck with a loud thump, before setting off at a run into the dark streets beyond.

How could he do this to me? I thought he was my friend, she thought as her feet pounded on the slabs of the pavement below.

But how could I have been so foolish? It was all a trap, all, always a trap....

The vampire ran into the night.

Back in the chaos of the apartment, the fight was short-lived, and brutal. Muzzle-fire strobed like club-land lights, and at some point the lights – or the electricity – were blown, resulting in moments of intense, blinding light and then deep darkness.

Snarls. White teeth. Roars of pain and anger.

Kaiden had to maintain his discipline to avoid what had happened last time. If he let go, if he let the abomination within take over, then surely he would end up rampaging through this entire warehouse block. There was nowhere for him to run, and he wanted to keep his wits about him, try to follow the vampire girl if he could.

But before he even had a chance to follow her, the door had burst open, and muzzle-fire was flashing. He hit the floor, rolling behind the small makeshift counter that served as his kitchen, returning shots with his own gun.

How could she do this to me? Run out on me? he found himself thinking, feeling hurt by the sudden lack of trust that the vampire had so callously shown him.

Before Kaiden could wonder if he really did blame her or not, he found himself being choked: whoever it was at the door had unleashed some sort of smoke grenade, and clouds of noxious, mustard- and pepper-based plumes filling his apartment in seconds, clogging his lungs and filling his nose. It felt like he was breathing sandpaper, and he couldn't see or breathe through the smoke.

The formula must have been specifically designed with Shifters and their kind in mind, as Kaiden found himself hacking and coughing, the sensitive pathways in his nose screaming in agony. He staggered, heading for any way out of the smoke.

He felt strong hands grab him by the shoulders and drag him, writhing and weak, out of his apartment. He was dragged the length of the corridor before he was dropped abruptly, and he couldn't feel any sensation in his face at all.

"Uggh?" he tried to growl, but his eyes were swelling up with whatever foul toxin they had put in.

"You just sit. Be good now," said a deep, guttural voice from above. Lubock. He had come here in person. The Alpha leader of the entire East Coast had actually entered the city, and all for him.

I should feel honoured, but instead, all I feel is in pain. Kaiden groaned. *Pain and anger.* He man hoped that the girl had gotten away.

The ones who had dragged him loomed into blurry view, their gas masks hanging from their faces. Overhead, the dark shadow of Lubock knelt down so that his face was close to Kaiden's own.

"Y'see, you failed to kill one of my patrol, Cerise? The lass with the braids? She came and told me about it, and when I heard that two of my Blood Dolls had been set upon by a freak that was half bat and half walking wolf, well, d'you know who I thought of? You saved a Leech. You brought her here, and when my patrol found you in the markets, your Leech-friends decided to burn the place to the ground."

"No. It's not like that," Kaiden murmured through the pain.

"No, it *won't* be like that," Lubok was growling as he raised himself up, and, it so happened, one large booted foot. "At first I wanted you torn limb from limb, and then I saw that you would be better use to me alive."

The boot came down, and, with a sudden stab of pain, Kaiden fell into darkness.

Meanwhile, elsewhere in the city, Tay ran. As an Elder, she could run for hours at a time with very little need to stop, pause, or breathe, and she found herself doing this. It was rare that she felt scared, but she did now.

Things were spiralling out of control. She couldn't quite remember what she was supposed to be doing, where, or with who.

It's the lack of a brood, or a crypt, she told herself, seeing another armoured personnel carrier at the end of a street, spilling out white-suited Servitors. *Damn!* She turned, sprinting down the nearest alleyway. She wasn't sure if they had heard her, or even seen her, but she knew that her superior Elder's reflexes would make sure that she could be much further away by the time they came to investigate.

She took the first exit on the block, ran through the slow-moving traffic, and down the alleyway opposite. Within a few minutes, she was far away from the last patrol.

Kaiden was right; there are Servitors everywhere, she thought as her feet pounded the pavement. Every couple of blocks there would be another personnel carrier stationed, with the surly Servitors standing around, smoking, or talking grimly to each other in hushed voices.

Tay had little reason to wonder why or how, as the air still smelled of burning and the smoke from the smouldering wreckage had now blackened the river side part of the Brooklyn skyline. *The Elders are going to be twitchy; they are going to be asking questions, expecting mortals to act up.*

She eventually stopped running when she felt even her virus-enhanced lungs starting to burn. She slowed down, gasping, finding that her legs had taken her almost to the waterfront, near the old bridge. From up here she could look down to where the mortal markets had been. Usually at this time of the night, they would be lit with the chaos of unregulated lighting; strips of Christmas lights next to gas lamps, near mobile generator-fed strip lights. It had always appeared pretty to her in the night, like a permanent New Year's Eve party.

Now, however, most of it was dark, and the foot crowds amassed around the bridge were large. Tay pulled up her collar and kept her pale face low as she tried to squeeze through. Around her, subconsciously, the mortals nearest her started to pull themselves away as their primal prey sense was triggered. *One of the added benefits of being an undead devourer of the living*, Tay thought to herself.

Still, however, the crowds were heavy, and did not part easily around her. Soon she was surrounded by other fearful travellers attempting to get to the checkpoint that would access Manhattan.

Tay risked a glance upwards. The checkpoint was double-guarded, Servitors in their pale suits standing on the small gantry way over the gates, checking passes as they let people through.

I don't have a pass. I don't even have a wallet. Tay felt mild panic rise in her, and clenched her jaws to try to quiet it down. She waited patiently until there were only a few humans ahead of her, and then, mentally apologising for what she was about to do, she let her incisors fall forward, and hissed loudly.

"Agh!" Wails from around her as the mortals jumped in shock. They hadn't been aware that they had been so near one of their 'masters'. *And they have no way of telling that I'm a Feral*, she thought happily to herself as she put on an angry, accusative glare and scowled around her.

"What is the meaning of this!?" She put on her best, haughtiest voice, (doing a subtle impersonation of Jeremiah when he was angry, she thought), and tried to add a hint of a European lilt to her tone. The older European lineages of vampires always got more respect. "Do I have to wait here like cattle?" she declared loudly.

Two of the mortals nearest to her even fell to their knees, heads bowed in supplication. She sneered at them, gently prodding one with her boot.

I'm so sorry, she thought, but didn't let her guilt reach her features. Instead she gave a more angered hissing snarl, causing the remaining mortals between her and the gate to scramble backwards.

The Servitors are going to be harder to impress, she thought, keeping her back straight and her eyes forward as she strode purposefully forward towards the gate. She didn't stop until it was obvious that the Servitors *weren't* going to open the gate to her, and she arched an eyebrow and pulled herself up short with a gasp.

"What in the eternal night are you doing?" she demanded of the nearest, fixing him with the full power of her glare.

The poor Servitor looked almost as pale as his uniform as he faced the wrath of an Elder fully directed at him. Tay knew that if she wasn't a Feral, then just at a mere snap of her fingers she could have him dumped into the river below, or bound up and delivered to a sanctuary of her choosing. Such was the dark power that the Elder Kindred had over their mortal serfs.

"Uh-uh... it's orders, ma'am..." the young man stuttered.

"Orders!?" Tay barked at him, letting the virus flush her with strength, and her pupils dilate with predatory intent. A tingling, almost electric sensation started to ooze through her veins. "I'm sorry, but did *I* give you orders? Unless I am very much mistaken, I do not believe that I did!" she hissed, turning back to the gate, as if fully expecting to be obeyed.

To the Servitor's credit, he tried to raise his hand to stop her, but instead put it on the gate, and was half unlocking it when he paused again.

"It's just, your ladyship, we have a list of all of the kindred in Archon Jeremiah's territory, and we usually ask permission to register your name..." he muttered.

"Permission? Registers? Orders?" Tay laughed, her voice louder and echoing deeper than she would ever naturally do herself. "These things are not for me. Now I'll tell Jeremiah just how good you've been. A very good little guard!" She put the last part in her baby-pet voice, as if talking to a beloved animal, and saw the guard looking pleased, then nervous, then confused.

"Well?" Tay snapped.

"Ah, yes, of course ma'am." The mortal swiped his key-card against the gate, and with a loud creaking noise, it swung open and the Feral stepped through.

Thank the night. Just keep walking, keep walking. Tay kept up a fast pace, ignoring the silence behind her as the Servitors watched her go with mollified glances. When she had already stalked a good twenty feet, she heard a distant human voice calling.

"Excuse me? Ma'am?"

Just keep walking. Ignore them like it is nothing to do with you. You are an Elder. You don't pay attention to these animals.

Tay regretted the thought, but she needed the resolution to keep on her fast-paced stalk. The Servitor guard called again, but by then the crowd of mortals were starting to murmur once more ahead of the gate, upset by being so easily upstaged by a seemingly 'undercover' Elder, and the Servitors had far more important things on their mind. Tay heard shouts behind her as the mortals started expressing their fear and outrage.

Everybody wants to get out of Brooklyn after the market attack, even just for a few nights, Tay thought as she kept up her brisk pace. She didn't blame them – the streets looked as full as they did when a cull was about to take place. Much safer to keep your head down and hide.

I wonder how long it will take before Jeremiah hears of my passing into another Archon's territory? Tay thought as she neared the other side of the bridge.

This side of the river was much more brightly-lit, with billboards and advertising screens glowing over distant downtown. The streets nearest the river (and the bridge to the market) were a little quieter, almost deserted as the residents of Manhattan wanted to distance themselves as much as possible from the events of their neighbourhood. It felt to Tay like wandering into another country, and she imagined what it must be like for both the Elders and the mortals here – slowly watching Brooklyn tear itself apart.

How can they stand by and do nothing as Jeremiah firebombs a whole district? What are they thinking?

As it turned out, Tay only got a couple of streets into Manhattan when she got the chance to find out as a black limousine screeched to a halt in front of her, and the shaded window rolled down.

"Tay Maslov? If you please..." One of the side doors opened, and Tay climbed inside.

"You know, Jackson, I didn't expect you to send a car out for me," Tay was saying over a martini. Of course the full-blooded Elders didn't have to drink or eat, and many preferred to forgo the sham at all, but Tay was still a relatively 'young' vampire, and the desire for social acceptance was still strong.

She could still eat and drink, but would only result in being sick later. It was one of the facts that she missed most, being one of the 'undead'.

Tay Maslov stood at the bar next to a man in a scintillating suit of night purples and blues. His hair was short and dreaded into tiny tufts, and even in this dark and neon environment he wore a pair of expensive sunglasses.

He was forever the stylist, Jackson, Tay thought, watching her old friend twirl his cane at his side, keeping one eye on his waiters and the Blood Dolls in the corner of the bar. He had built this place from the ground up, buying it off of some mortal, and turning it into a successful – but elite – Blood Bar, with a very strict membership policy. The Dolls and Brothers that were allowed in were all of the most immaculate skin and scintillating personalities. He rejected dozens of applications from mortals all of the time. Elders, of course, had no trouble getting in.

Here he served a variety of spiced, flavoured, and mildly-drugged blood, as well as the selection of Blood Dolls and Brothers. Public feeding of live hosts wasn't exactly forbidden, but it was frowned upon by polite Elder society. Instead, the Blood Dolls and Brothers would draw the velvet curtains around the booths with their Elder companions; giggles and gasps would be heard on the other side, and only silhouettes seen.

For Tay and Jackson, however, they existed in the main lobby area of the cellar bar, standing with a few other lost souls under dim blue and orange lights, nursing their drinks.

"Well, I have my men watching the bridges. Have done ever since your Archon went crazy and started firing his own turf!" Jackson laughed, a warm, rich sound compared to many of the other Elders that she knew.

"Yeah. You could say that life is getting pretty complicated over there." Tay sniffed her martini, frowning. She wondered if Kaiden had gotten out of there alive. She wondered what his plan had been all along. She couldn't quite shake the feeling that there must be some reason he hadn't tried harder to stop her leaving.

What if he was telling the truth, and he wasn't friends with Lubok?

"Hello? Tay?" Jackson prodded her with his cane, snickering. "You look like you've seen a ghost!"

"No, just... There is trouble over there. Something big is going down, and I'm not sure what..."

"Oh, you mean apart from you being turned Feral by your ex?" Jackson said sharply.

Tay felt a shiver of fear pass over her. "You heard, then."

The nightclub vampire sighed dramatically, turning to signal for one of his Blood Dolls to bring him a glass of blood. "Of course I did. Your name appeared on the message that was sent out across the city. You and a few others that Jeremiah is now pursuing. You have been cast out, and cast down."

Tay set her martini down on the counter, very, very silently. "How long do you think I have?" she asked softly, trying to remember any safe hideouts in Manhattan.

"Not long. Archon Bethania here is a little different that yours over there. She's actually competent, for one thing." Jackson remained smiling and jovial, as though it was all a big joke.

Of course he would; he was around when alcohol was still in prohibition. He was trying to bootleg alcohol to the mortals, whilst supplying blood to the Elders. He's seen it all come and go, Tay. *A bit of trouble never bothers a creature like Jackson.*

"So I guess I should get moving then?" she groaned, looking up. "You couldn't help an old friend out, could you? Let me know any good places for Ferals on this side of the river?"

Jackson slapped the table and laughed at the same time. "I do, and, no, I'm not going to tell you, because I like you too much."

"What? If you liked me, Jackson, you'd help me get out of the city!" Tay said, her voice a little loud even for the bar. "You know what Jeremiah is like…"

"Like you said, it looks like Archon Jeremiah has got quite a lot on his plate already." Jackson was grinning. "He's not the one you have to worry about. It's Archon Bethania."

Tay grunted in frustration. "So, what, you're just going to throw me to the wolves?"

"Not at all. Like *I* said, I *like* you, kid; you've got guts – and that is why the only thing that I am going to help you with is getting an audience with Bethania, and you can explain to her all your troubles. She is the only one who can help you."

"You mean try to get my Feral status revoked," Tay said, "which can only be done by another Archon."

"Exactly – and I don't see Jeremiah lining up to do it. Is he?" Jackson signalled for another drink. "Now, let me make some calls, and we'll see if we can get you a spot with her highness." The vampire chuckled.

I wish I could be as relaxed as he is. Tay scowled, watching him as he stalked off to the offices of the cellar bar. *I should just flee now.* She looked at the doorway. *I should run out of here and never look back – keep on running until everyone I've ever known forgets me, and I even forget my own name...*

For a moment, Tay had a distinct sensation of sunlight on her eyes, forest scents, and the crunch of moss and earth underfoot. She wanted to be home, she realized, far away.

Odd. I haven't called that place home in a long while. Tay thought about her childhood upbringing, back when she was a mortal. Somehow in her mind, the memory of her past had become entwined with the earthy, wood-smoke smell of the man who had saved her life. Kaiden.

If he had wanted to kill me – why didn't he just do it when I was asleep? Why did he get some clean blood to strengthen me up again? She found herself thinking as a pretty young Blood Doll walked up to her, blonde hair tied in pigtails.

"Your ladyship?" the mortal said, her skin painted with a heavy white foundation, and her eyes looking sunken and tired on the other side. "Do you require company tonight, ma'am?" she said in a small voice.

"No." Tay shook her head quickly. The thought of live-feeding here, now, suddenly made her feel sick. Looking hurt, the Blood Doll backed away to try her luck at another patron of Jackson's establishment.

What is wrong with me? Tay thought. *Since going Feral, since I found out that I couldn't trust Jeremiah, it seems that I have lost the appetite for it...*

"Ah, my little Tay," Jackson said loudly, completely ignoring the groupies and mortals around him. "You are in luck. Archon Bethania is wasting no time, it seems. You're to see her this very night!"

Tay couldn't be certain if the vampire was chuckling with joy, or in ridicule.

But what can I do?

7. Loyalty

"Father Sky, keep me quick; send me winds of thought and clear sight; Mother Earth, make me strong, promise me meat and a warm place to lay my head. All else, I will hunt for myself."

- *Three-Feathers (Poems of a Shifter Pack)*

When Kaiden opened his eyes, it was to leaves, rocks, and woods.

"Ugh," he groaned. His head was pounding, and it felt like he had been run through the wringer. Slowly, the man started to run through his mental checklist: breathing, heartrate. He flexed his fingers, his toes, moved his legs and arms.

Nothing broken then, and everything still where it was when I woke up this morning. Kaiden supposed, considering his current position, that was probably the best that he could ask for.

But how did I get out of the city? Out here? He opened his eyes, seeing stars in the sky, blinking between the dark shadows of trees. He took a deep breath, smelling forest moss, earth, and nature. No gasoline, no smog, no exhaust.

The man knew perfectly well that the nearest wild lands nearest to the city must be an hour away, the tip of New York State, up the coast towards the hills and the woods. Kaiden knew, because he had spent a considerable amount of time there. It had been his parents' territory.

No. Kaiden knew that there was something about the air, something that smelled and felt familiar. A gentle fragrance that he had thought he had forgotten.

Home. It was obvious now that he thought about it. He swore at the thought of Lubock. Why was he doing this? Why did he bring him *here* of all places, out to where his parents had been killed?

Where Kaiden himself had been brought up. A ranch in the woods.

Kaiden got to his feet almost without realizing, not feeling the chill on his skin of the before-dawn air. He still had on his torn and bloodied clothes that he had been wearing in the firefight, but he didn't feel cold or uncomfortable at all. Ahead of him, his feet started to track the way that they always had done in the past.

His feet found the overgrown lane that led through the woods, the forestry conservation woods that had all been chopped down for wooden planks had now re-sprouted, and the Sitka Spruce stood just seven or eight feet tall, spindly, and their minimal branches dark even against the sky. The path underfoot had once been gravel, with a ditch to one side and a fence, but the fence had fallen or been pulled down, and the ditch was nothing more than an overgrown riot of bushes and briars.

But the woods are quiet now. The woods are quiet, Kaiden found himself thinking. There were no sounds of the night-time rustlings of birds, or the distant barks of foxes, calls of wildcats or owls.

It was an unearthly quiet, the sort of stillness that only occurred after the animals of the forest had been frightened, badly.

Just like they were frightened the night that the Elders came for my parents. Kaiden tried not to remember, his hands balling at his sides.

Slowly, his feet started trudging forward, certain, determined. The gravel path now had a blanket of moss over it, but it still moved in the same direction. It always moved in the same direction. It curved around the bend in the land, the trees abruptly stopping to reveal a small corral against the forestry. Kaiden's parents had been wardens of the park here, helping to protect the woodland, re-plant the trees, and instruct the logging companies that came up every year.

Had been, Kaiden thought. There hadn't even been enough left to bury them after the Elders were through with them.

The man raised his eyes to what was ahead of him. The house where he had grown up was no longer, by any standards, a house. It was, in fact, a ruin of two and a half walls, mostly held up by ivy, and, Kaiden knew, underneath the ivy there would be scorch marks. The entire building was burnt underneath the shadowed ivy. It was a blackened remnant of its former self.

Holes in the walls could once have been windows, their sharp edges softened by the wild, and the eaves of the roof were no longer straight lines, but crowded with saplings. New things had come to live here, and Kaiden remembered.

He was young when the Elders came, just half way through his teens, gangly and perennially annoyed. He worked in the forest with his father and mother when he could, or hitched a ride over to the neighbours' ranches and farms. He had known that his parents were Shifters from an early age, almost from the crib. Out here on the edge of the wild, the tricky part of growing up was not accepting what sort of creatures his parents were, but, in fact, accepting what the other mortals were not.

As a rule, the Shifter communities, packs, and tribes kept away from the cities. They preferred to live more natural lives, living as close to the earth and the sunlight as they could allow.

Perhaps it was a reaction against the way that the Elders lived, in their underground bunkers, poisoning the very air to make the world more perennially night-lit, Kaiden thought.

Over the centuries, he was told the two species had held a very uneasy sort of truce. Every now and again the Elders would try to cull the Shifters, sending out armies or helicopters or whatever they had to destroy the wild communities of the strange people. And every year they failed.

They would kill hundreds, drive even more away from their homes, disrupt the bloodlines for a generation, but the Shifters were tough. The Shifters were resilient, and they had the added advantage of being out in the wild, as far from civilisation as possible. Out here, it wasn't easy for an Elder to always find somewhere dark before sunrise; even the weakest and newest of the Elders who could withstand the sun in small doses still suffered nausea and headaches, sun-burn and confusion in the sun. That is why the Elders relied on Servitors, and why they could never push their advantage against the Shifters for too long.

What did you do against an enemy that could always retreat into the mountains and wild places of the world?

The Shifters, however, had the disadvantage of their own virus. When they were angry it caused them to mutate, to assume the shape of their virus subspecies (coyote, wolf, dog, cat, lion, bear, fox, rat, and so on), and that meant that most of them gave up technology in times of stress. Electronically locked metal doors became impenetrable barriers. Getting angry in line at a coffee-shop resulted in a witch-hunt and a cull. Most Shifters detached as much as possible from society – favouring hard cash or payment in kind over banks (because then they wouldn't have to risk visiting the cities).

The Shifters were poor, and they lacked the firepower and technology (and the numbers) to pose a serious threat to the Elders. (For a start, they would have to find a way to retake the cities, and all of the Servitors and the mortals inside).

Instead, things like what was before Kaiden happened, sneaky raids in the middle of the night by Elders at the easiest targets of Shifters nearby.

Sometimes the Shifters retaliated, sending packs into the cities to find and kill a sanctuary of Elders or an Archon if they could manage it. They almost always entirely could not, leaving the Elders with the upper hand.

Kaiden still remembered the night. He had been awakened by his father, who had put a hand over his mouth and told him to be quiet.

"Get to the cubbyhole. Hide until it's clear, then run. Run as far and as fast as you can, you hear me, Kay?" In Kaiden's memory, his father was tall and immeasurably austere, but now, the man knew that he was just scared. He had only been about ten years older than Kaiden was now at the time of his death, Kaiden realized.

He had blondish hair, perpetual stubble.

Kaiden had eased on his clothes, not saying a word as he saw his mother appear in the doorway, a shotgun in her hand. No one had to say or explain anything to him; it was obvious. There were no sounds coming from the windows that they kept open all night. His family had always preferred to listen to the sounds of the forest to lull them to sleep, and now its lack might have saved their son's life.

"But I can help! I can fight!" Kaiden had said, puffing himself up after he had his jeans and camo jacket and boots on.

"No, Kay." This from his auburn-haired mother. "You know why. You can't Shift. You may never be able to; I'm sorry, but just do as your father says…"

Kaiden didn't remember if he protested more after that; all he remembered next was sitting crouched in the wooden, reinforced cubbyhole that his father had built under the floor and down into the ground. Sound echoed from above, mutated, and became muffled.

Shouts. Roars. The booming sound of a shotgun going off, a sound like tearing paper, and the smell of fire.

Next came the screams.

In the present day, Kaiden was shaking with emotion. He remembered crawling out of that cubbyhole when he could feel the heat on his back. He had been too scared to move, and wishing desperately that at any moment his parents would arrive to open the hatch and haul him out – but they never came. No one ever came for him.

When the teenager crawled out of there, he found his home already burning, and the bodies of Elders and Servitors everywhere scattered in the dirt, dismembered, torn apart. Great scratch marks like the swipes of massive claws marred the walls and the ground, but they did not stop the terrible fate that had met his parents.

Their bodies burnt inside the hottest part of the fire.

"This is where they were," a growling voice said from the darkness, and Kaiden jumped, snarling.

I should have known this was the reason. Kaiden saw the immense form of Lubock, the leader of the East Coast tribe and all of its packs, step out from the wreckage of his home. *My home.* Kaiden felt himself growling, but Lubock ignored him, and just kept on talking.

"Did you know that we were the ones to clean up this place? My pack and I?" Lubock said, kicking aside some of the broken masonry underfoot, exposing burnt tiles. He was a big man with wild, dark hair, looking like a figure out of a Russian fairy tale.

"My pack was the first here in the morning. We came as soon as we smelled the smoke on the breeze. We spent three days mourning your parents, adding wood to the flames so that their funeral pyre would be seen for miles around," Lubock said, his voice distant. "Many more Shifters came, and they paid their respects to the fire. They swore revenge for this crime."

The chieftain looked up at Kaiden, and his large, dark eyes were like the night itself. "But you never came, Kaiden. You had already stolen away to the city, about to fall in with the Professor, swearing your own revenge against the Elders. You never had a chance to say goodbye to your parents in the proper Shifter way."

"Maybe it's because I'm not a Shifter," Kaiden found himself saying, throwing the words out like an accusation.

If I had been, if I could have shifted – if I had the powers that I had now – then surely I could have saved my parents, Kaiden thought again, automatically, just as he had thought on and off for the years that had passed since the incident.

"But you are, Kaiden," Lubock growled. "Or were, at any rate. Do you know so little of your heritage?"

"Look, I don't have time for this." Kaiden started to circle the bigger Shifter, hunching his shoulders. "Is this what you wanted, to bring me here to finish off the job that the Elders started?" he barked.

"Pup!" Lubock moved quicker than a striking snake, vaulting across the handful of metres that separated them and backhanding him across the cheek. Not enough to draw blood, but enough to send him spinning to the ground. Kaiden's head spun with the force of it.

"How dare you say that of me, comparing my methods to the Leeches!" Lubock snarled, obviously deeply offended. "That will be your only warning. You never learned all of our ways because the Professor decided not to. He decided to make you his experiment, but you *are* a Shifter, even if you don't know it. All of the families of those who change are Shifters. Their genes might not be as strong as some, but they still hold it. The Shifters *always* respect family, pack, and tribe, because without them we are nothing. Do you understand me?" Lubock's voice grew louder until it ended in a roar.

Kaiden looked up from his crouch. *No,* he thought, *I don't understand you. Why bring me here? Why make me see this terrible place again?* "Why attack me in New York, drug me, and drag me out here if you only wanted to lecture me about family?" he growled, hurting. Kaiden could feel the dark weight of something pressing against his eyes, a memory of the hurt that he had as a child that he never wanted to revisit again.

Lubock was almost standing over him, a dark shadow against the sky. "I am not here to *lecture* you, Kaiden. I am here on behalf of the memory of your parents, to try to *save* you."

"*You* want to *save* me?" Kaiden spat. "I seem to recall that just recently you wanted to kill me for being an abomination."

The face of the East Coast tribe leader was in shadow, so Kaiden couldn't see the expression that he was pulling, only the silence that followed his question. After what seemed like a long while, Lubock let out a deep sigh.

"Kaiden, I have come to realize that it is not entirely your fault that you are an abomination."

"Oh great, thanks," Kaiden bristled.

"And there are many betas in my own pack that want nothing more than to see you torn limb from limb. You've killed Shifters; in the laboratory, you killed the Professor – and, as you know, that is a crime that cannot be forgotten."

"Blood is paid in blood," Kaiden found himself murmuring, reciting the old litany; one of the few things that his parents had the opportunity to teach him before they were hunted themselves and killed. They had told him it meant that if he ever gives his word, then he must stick to it, and if he is ever wronged, then he must defend himself.

"Yes. Blood is paid in blood. I cannot change that. You will have to answer for your crimes," Lubock said heavily. "But you are still Shifter, and you can still aid our cause."

"That is what I have been *trying* to do, Lubock." Kaiden half rose from his crouch, only to freeze when the larger pack leader whirled towards him, anger clear on his face.

"By getting two of my own killed in the market today? By saving some Feral Leech the night before? *How* have you been helping me, Kaiden? Because it looks like you have already chosen your side."

Now it was Kaiden's turn to sputter with anger as he felt the heat spread through his muscles like a wave. With a thought, his muscles were mutating and merging as he leapt across the short space, reaching for Lubock with hands that were now claws, and arms that were thick knots of furred flesh. He felt pain erupt from his face and his shoulders, as leathery, bat-like wings started to unfurl, and from his face a snout, bristling with teeth...

"Gargh!" Lubock was changing just as quickly, rolling in the dirt now as an eight-feet-tall wolf-man, his snout cross-hatched with white scars as thick as a human's finger, his fur a mottled black, shot through with a wiry grey, and his claws old and cracked. But still, he was strong, and fast. He caught the creature that Kaiden had turned into and they rolled together, Kaiden mindlessly snapping at Lubock's throat, while the pack leader growled and held him back, his own arms quivering.

Kaiden didn't know how strong he was, and it was only his untrained fury that set him at a disadvantage, as the bigger werewolf managed to flip him over onto his back, uncomfortably sitting atop him, his legs and forearms pushing down on the beast's leathery wings.

Kaiden waited for the inevitable to happen, the killing bite that would tear out his throat.

It never came. Lubock just remained atop him, panting.

"Stop this, Kaiden. I am not here to kill you," he growled, his mouth barely forming the words.

The abomination felt a new sensation; fear. Its nose was filled with the dirt of the soil of his old home, and, with it, the smell of soot and burning. The smell of the old fire filled up his mind as he remembered the heat pressing down on his back, the sound of distant screams and gunshots...

The abomination started to writhe and shake, his muscles spasming as Kaiden once again assumed his human shape, panting.

"Good. So you can come out of it," Lubock said grimly, his voice once again human as he jumped lightly away. He was panting and breathing heavily, the exertion plain in his face.

"Why?" When Kaiden spoke, his voice was ragged, his rage gone. He didn't understand what was happening to him, or why.

"Because you need to know, Kaiden. You need to know why we fight the way we do – and we need you on our side," Lubock said grimly. "If this is true, and you have some connection to the Leechesother, then – then your..." Lubock looked distinctly sick as he forced himself to say it, "your need to *dream* may be able to help the Shifters. Help us avenge your family!"

A thought struck Kaiden. "The rest don't know, do they? The other pack leaders. The alphas."

Lubock's eyes narrowed as he re-appraised the strange creature on the ground. "You are quick, Kaiden, but then, so were your parents. No. They think you have turned traitor to us all, and want the blood price paid for your crimes. But there is something big coming, a plan in motion that can help the Shifters finally, once and for all, drive the Leeches out of the city – and I have realized that we cannot have you running around, choosing sides as you will."

"I never changed sides!" Kaiden tried to say again, but Lubock wasn't listening.

"This is the deal, Kaiden, use your... *unique* talents on our side, or we will make sure you won't be able to interfere in this fight. Or this war."

"You'll kill me now. Here," Kaiden saw.

The pack leader nodded. Kaiden wondered if he could take him if it came to a real fight. He wondered if he was strong enough, quick enough. He might be. But, then again, he might not.

"There's this one Leech I know. A girl. She might be able to help us," Kaiden said, his voice low. *Why can I not shake the feeling that I'm betraying her?* the abomination found himself thinking. *What was this new plan of Lubock's? The drug? Infect all the Blood Dolls in the city? Start another war?*

8. Betrayal

"The Archon system is one of the oldest ruling principles of the predatory society. The oldest vampire will be named Archon; powerful and wise above all others. But to have one such head in control over such a large body proved dangerous – as we know, heads can easily be cut off! So the Archon system was instituted, 'councils' of leaders, highly territorial, each controlling their own district. Thus it will be hard to ever rid ourselves of this Lych menace – we will wipe out one nest, only for another district to take over!"

- The Helsing Talks, (BANNED)

Archon Bethania, the oldest Elder in the district of Manhattan, did not make a secret of where her own Sanctuary was. Tay wasn't surprised when she was driven through the crowded streets with purple-suited Jackson at her side, to find that the sanctuary of perhaps the most powerful vampire in all of New York was surrounded by crowds.

Their black stretch-limousine crawled in front of the large theatre building, with its blazing coloured lights declaring the latest show. The crowds of mortals, Servitors, Blood Dolls, and Brothers mixed freely here, each seemingly excited and a little intoxicated about tonight's entertainment.

"Ah, she's always run an open house, our Bethania," Jackson laughed, tapping on the window at a group of Blood Dolls who were shouting and waving at their car. Only the Elders had the resources to be able to afford limousines. *And only the Elders could afford to run a place like this!* Tay thought, almost as an afterthought, as she peered past the heads of the mortals outside to the theatre.

The letters were picked out in flash-bulbs, mostly off-yellow, but occasionally blazing red, crimson, white.

VAUDEVILLE. BURLESQUE. THE GLORY OF TRAGEDY.

Tay shivered as she saw the large, wall-sized posters. There were depictions of women in skimpy outfits swinging from trapezes, or of Blood Dolls engaged in bizarre performances of burlesque dreaming. Archon Bethania apparently had transformed the usually secretive, private *(even intimate,* Tay thought) act of the blood bars into a district obsession. She gave the mortals, Elders, and the Blood servitors what they wanted by turning the act of *dreaming* into a spectator sport, an entertainment for titillation or horror for the masses.

Tay wondered just how many of the 'normal' mortals in the audience would go home unaffected by morning. Or whether they would all make it home at all. *This is a theatre of cruelty. A theatre of the absurd,* she thought, realizing strangeness of it. All of the humans mortals who were arriving here were effectively *food* for the rich Elders, and they were willingly, laughingly, seducingly, throwing themselves into the dinner – and paying for the privilege!

"Well, you couldn't get people to pay to be near Archon Jeremiah, that's for certain," Tay said,

"Ha! That's true!" Jackson was laughing. "And you know why? That Elder is a bore!" he said, and Tay gasped at the scandalous nature of his assertion. In Brooklyn, even if another Elder were to speak out against their Archon, Jeremiah would almost certainly have them pronounced Feral. Loyalty is everything.

"Oh, don't look so shocked. You've all been thinking it over the water!" Jackson was snickering as the limousine very slowly negotiated the turn in the road and started to edge down the side of the grand Sanctuary-Theatre. "Archon Jeremiah is a bore," he repeated. "He throws his servitors around, clamps down on this or that, is cruel, and vicious. Yawn. What's new?" Jackson made an impression of yawning. "He has no finesse, and no style. Who would pay to be in his company? Archon Bethania, on the other hand..." Jackson waggled his eyebrows above his dark sunglasses. "She has glamour. She has mystery. She throws a show before she sits down to feast. She tells her mortals how beautiful and discerning they are before she takes the money from their pockets and the blood from their veins. You have to remember, young Tay, that you are still a young kindred, and have a lot to learn about our ways."

"I guess you're right..." Tay found herself saying.

"Archon Bethania has spent a long time rising to the top, and she knows how to work the mortal population. So long as you give them something to reach for, they'll do anything for you. Even if you are only offering them the sight of another person's downfall, they'll gladly take it, and count themselves lucky!" Jackson laughed his loud, chortling bray.

The limousine slid past an opening garage door and into an underground parking lot, seemingly underneath the theatre itself. Tay saw lights from concrete walls, other limousines, Mercedes cars, Servitor drivers and footmen standing by their charges. They found a place to park and, as soon as they stepped outside, Tay could hear the pounding beat of some bass-like music above.

"Welcome to the Bacchanal, my little Tay." Jackson was already pointing the way to a set of lifts where other Elders and their servitors were already coming and going. The club-owning vampire swept Tay in beside him, and they waited until the lift 'dinged' musically and started to rise.

"Uh, are you sure that this is going to be okay? I am, after all, Feral," Tay said, looking at the burnished mirror walls and the deep carpet of the lift. *Even the lifts are opulent!* she thought.

Jackson chuckled, and told her not to worry about it. Yet.

I suppose that there's not much I can do anyway, even if this isn't all okay. Tay sighed.

The lift passed two more 'stops' where it didn't pause, and instead came to rest and opened its doors to an assault of light and music.

"Come on, toots." Jackson was taking Tay by the hand and leading her out into the main hall of the theatre space.

Sweet night! Tay could hardly believe her eyes as she followed her friend, narrowly avoiding being jostled by others. In here the Elders freely mingled with the mortals. There was always an air of devotion and respect, as Blood Dolls followed the small groups of Elders around the theatre space, but there were no armed guards (visible, anyway) or walls separating them.

But it wasn't just the social set-up that was overwhelming for the young vampire. The space itself was the most extravagant that she had ever seen. The room was a massive oval, and they emerged onto a high balcony of other lifts that swept down to one raised level of the hall, complete with leather booths and its own cocktail bar. A few steps inlaid with mother-of-pearl led down from there to a lower dancing area (polished wood gleaming as the swaying, lurching, shaking forms of Blood Dolls and Brothers came together and went). Tay gasped at some of the moves that she saw some of the people on the dancefloor pulling.

On the far side of the dancefloor, there was another raised area of seating and bars, and then beyond that a sort of arcade under another balcony, housing private, velvet-curtained booths. Next to the arcade was a small stage, currently occupied by gyrating and swaying dancers. It held its own backdrop of starry curtains and large, hanging moons to match their movements and costumes.

Opposite the dancefloor was the main stage, big enough for several houses and currently showcasing what seemed to be a complicated performance piece of dancing and acting. Rows of dancers dressed in pristine white where being hauled up into the heavens on wires, as others on stilts, dressed in black, danced and swung around beneath them. People roared with laughter, horror, and delight.

A third, smaller stage was near the far edge of the first bar, and this held what seemed to be a small band, playing stringed instruments. Tay caught a note every now and again, fighting to be heard over the band on the main performance stage.

"There must be hundreds, hundreds of people in here!" Tay gasped. She had never seen so many Elders and mortals all in the same space all at once. It was far more usual for Elders to isolate themselves and to only meet in small groups, lest some accident or attack befall them.

"Almost a thousand, I think," Jackson had to lean in to say to her as he pointed and laughed at another Elder dressed in a top hat and tails, nodding in his direction. "There! There's our queen!"

Tay looked at her friend as he said this; he seemed to acquire this breathless quality when talking about the Archon of Manhattan. Tay followed his eager face, to see a gaggle of people surrounding one of the private booths, Elders in suits next to the most elegant Blood Brothers and Dolls that she had ever seen, all eager for a moment's audience with the Archon.

"She holds her court out here? Amidst all this?" Tay was surprised.

"Well, little Tay, this *is* Manhattan – or did you forget?" Jackson led his charge by her elbow through the crowds, fielding advances of mortals and the blood bonded alike.

They passed through the streams of people – the mortals parting around them as they did around every Elder, and the Elders stepping aside as they registered who Jackson was leading into their sanctuary. A polite look of distaste, a smothered gasp, and the ripple of scandal spread out from them, and by the time Jackson had led her past the second and third stage to the booths in the arcade at the back, there were already sombre and sullen faces ready to greet him.

"Jackson," said an Elder, looking for all the world like a well-dressed, slick—haired dapper young businessman from the 1900s. He wore white gloves that were only a marginal shade lighter than his skin, and his eyes were an unnerving icy blue.

"Gatsby," Jackson nodded. "You know the rules, my man. Any Elder is allowed to attend open court. Anyone at all."

"Of course, my dear Jackson, but standards are standards, are they not? I mean..." The Elder 'Gatsby' raised his eyebrows towards Tay. "No insult meant, Madame, but I am sure that you understand...?"

Tay found herself starting to oblige the charming Elder socialite, about to say that of course she should retire and not bother the Archon – but Jackson's hand clamped around her wrist, painfully.

"Nonsense. Open court, Gatsby. Open. Court," his voice growled, and the younger-looking Elder held his gaze for a moment before breaking away with a sudden cough.

"Of course, my man. Of course." He nodded at Tay as they slipped past into the inner realm of the inner court of the Archon Bethania.

Tay heard a few hisses from the vampires, an intake of breath as doubtless some recognised – or guessed – who she must be. *Has word of my downfall spread so far already?* She gulped as she stepped forward.

The booth that Archon Bethania was currently occupying was the size of a small room, with a round table in the centre and a semi-circular red leather couch spread around it. Male and female Elders sat or stood leaning against the wood-lined walls, smoking cigarettes and looking at her with their long, paler-than-normal faces. Everyone was wearing their finest clothes, and none was finer than the woman who sat at the heart of the room.

The Archon Bethania wore an almost see-through cream slip that was loose against her white skin, and half a dozen strings of pearls hanging around her neck. Long, elbow-length satin gloves stretched from her fingers to her elbows, and her hair was short, black, and cut into a bob. She wore deep, dark eyeliner, and her lips were painted a deep royal purple.

"So, you are this Tay Maslov that I've been hearing about?" Archon Bethania casually tapped ash from her long cigarette on its holder onto a silver dish on the table.

"Your highness," Tay found herself saying, bowing her head.

"Hmm. Manners, I guess." Bethania looked bored, and barely older than Tay herself. Were it not for the darkness of her eyes or the way that her skin was tight and almost ephemeral, nothing would give away the fact that she was anything over her mid-thirties. "Ladies and gentlemen," Bethania performed a very soft, languid clap with her gloves, and immediately they started shuffling out of the booth, casting hisses and angry glances at Tay and Jackson.

"That means you, too, Jackson – you disreputable old rogue." Archon Bethania shooed Jackson away with her gloves. He looked affronted for a second, but then turned and left the booth-room without a sound, leaving Tay to Archon Bethania's scrutiny alone.

"He's terrible, isn't he?" the Archon sighed heavily. "He'll be the ruin of Manhattan, I swear. Come." The Archon tapped the velvet seat of the now-unoccupied coach. "You will sit, and answer my questions, Tay Maslov, of the brood of Archon Jeremiah."

In a vague sense of unreality, Tay did so. *Jeremiah has never treated me like this,* she thought. She wasn't exactly getting respect from the Archon – but, then again, she wasn't exactly getting outright condescension either. *Archon Jeremiah treated us all like his slaves – whether we were vampires, his brood, or not!*

As if reading her mind – which, Tay realized, might not actually be beyond the realm of possibility for an Archon – Bethania smiled a thin-lipped smile at her.

"No, you will find me very different from Archon Jeremiah. He is still young, bless. He doesn't really understand what he is yet."

"What he is, ma'am?" Tay found her voice and croaked. She thought it patently obvious.

Bethania laughed, a sound like the bells of a funeral service. "Oh, of course, you are young as well, aren't you? Of course you all *think* that you are vampires – stalking around in the night, here to feed on the mortals, blood makes right, and all that…" Her laugh tinkled again, making Tay shiver.

"But you are both young. Jeremiah thinks that it is his right to torment the mortals underneath him. He thinks that he is an apex predator, when, really, nothing could be further from the truth." Bethania took another long drag from her cigarette, before filling the space between them with its sweet smoke like treacle. "Think about our life-cycle, child. We are vampires; we are called Elders for a reason. Did you know that the average life-span of an Elder is around two hundred years? Incredible, isn't it? Now, the average lifespan of a mortal is eighty years, seventy in most poorer cases. What can you infer from that?" Bethania fixed her with a critical eye.

"That – that we shouldn't be bothered by the present?" Tay took a wild guess.

Bethania barked a laugh once more; short, sharp, and cruel. "No. Quite the opposite. That we should be immediately and irreparably concerned about the present! The troubles to a mortal generation could make them give up, could make them go to war, could make them pass on dangerous ideas to their children, or pass on more chance of success. We Elders do not have long to get this right. We cannot merely forget an entire generation or type of people, thinking that life always goes on because we seem to!"

Tay nodded, although she didn't really see.

"Elders aren't predators, or rather, we aren't *just* predators. We're like shepherds. We have to guide and grow our flock, not allow the *wolves,*" the Archon added a slight growl to her voice as she said this, "to take them all. Or firebomb them out of existence. You see?"

Ah. Bethania was angry with Jeremiah about his market action. Tay understood. "The mortal markets."

"Yes. Precisely. Now, I have heard a little from my people over in Brooklyn what happened – now why don't *you* tell me what you think happened? I really don't have to tell you that the other Archons of the city, Maximus, Seb, and Huafei are *very* interested in what has been happening in Brooklyn, and why a pall of smoke is now obscuring half of New York City."

Tay opened and shut her mouth. *How much should I say? Should I tell them about the man who saved me? Will Archon Bethania be able to read my mind anyway?*

When Tay finished her narrative, she carefully set the last words down between them, and looked up.

"And that is how I came to be here."

There were several times when the Archon Bethania narrowed her eyes during the tale, her gentle nodding stopping and being replaced by a more inquisitive look (*like a cat*, Tay thought). But she did not say anything about the glaring holes in Tay's narrative – how Tay had been mysteriously wandering the streets after her 'outing' as a feral, and had heard about the firing of the market from a mutual friend. She didn't mention Kaiden.

Traitor, the vampire found herself thinking, and then couldn't quite work out if she meant Kaiden for the Shifter attack, or herself for not telling the Archon about him.

I mean, he must be important to all this, isn't he? He was a Shifter, and he said that he knew Shifters...

"And there's more," Tay finally blurted out.

Bethania said nothing, but raised an eyebrow.

"I-I heard from some other Ferals that there were Shifters in the city itself. A pack. That their leader, Lubok, has got something planned."

"This is the same Lubock who poisoned you?" Bethania asked, the first question that she had asked of her since Tay had begun her narrative.

"Yes. He's a Shifter leader I think – a werewolf," Tay said.

"And *how* did you come to know that *he* was the one who poisoned you through the Blood Dolls? Couldn't those particular Dolls just have an unhealthy addiction to something? And you, being a Feral, were too hungry to care about how you fed?" the Archon said, and her tone was precariously light and casual.

Damn. She's onto me. She knows that I'm holding back from her. Tay felt chilled as she blurted, "They told me. The Blood Dolls did. They revealed who they were as soon as I stopped *dreaming.* When I realized that it was all wrong and I was weak... They laughed at me and told me that their leader was a shifter named Lubock, and that he was seeding the city with these infected Blood Dolls of his..."

"And yet you still managed to fight them off, even in your weakened state. Very admirable," Bethania said, and when Tay was about to protest, to concoct an even greater story surrounding her miraculous escape, the Archon was already turning away.

"Never mind, dear. That is all that I need to hear. It is obvious to me that Jeremiah is acting a little *rashly* perhaps, and that the other Archons will have to *impress* upon him to be more careful." The woman looked into the middle distance, her eyes narrowed. "You are right to inform us of this matter of the infected Blood Dolls, and the Shifters. We shall have to pay a little more attention to what is going in and out of them, yes?"

"Uh, yes," Tay said, she had the sense of waiting for something. "So, if I may ask, Archon Bethania – am I accepted back into the kindred? Am I still Feral?"

"What? Oh, yes. I was rather thinking on that – that it might be more useful to us if we kept your restored position to ourselves, wouldn't you say?" The Archon Bethania was already looking around to see where the next drink might be coming from.

"Uh, I'm sorry Archon, but I don't quite follow. My restored position? Us?" Tay felt like she was wading through quicksand, and quickly about to fall through.

"Yes. Us being the other four Archons of this city. Thank you for all of your work and all that, but, you know, the survival of the species and all that, dear."

"What?" Tay felt the floor underneath her wobble. *Was Bethania throwing her to the wolves – literally?*

Bethania gave her one of her thin-lipped smiles. "I was all in favour of restoring you, you see, but, rather, seeing what you said about this Lubock character and these drugged up Blood Dolls – I think that we may just be able to use your current, ah, social disadvantage."

"I'm sorry, my lady, I don't follow."

The Archon was starting to look tired. "Look, it really is very simple. There must be a way that the Shifters are smuggling *their* Blood Dolls into the city, and testing the drug when they have the chance. My bet is through the Feral network – the other poor things in your position. So, what I will propose to do is send you to them as my sort of *ambassador*, and you will find out what you can about any new Blood Dolls or strange people offering new drugs to starving vampires!" Bethania looked very pleased with herself.

"But... some of the Ferals are little more than monsters. They'll try to feed on me, given half the chance!" Tay was mortified. "And what about Archon Jeremiah? You might need me to negotiate with him; he knows me..."

The look that Bethania used on her was enough to silence the younger vampire. "Tay. Please, don't embarrass yourself. I am an Archon, Jeremiah is an Archon, and considerably younger than me. We will be able to talk to each other. However, if you can find me some solid evidence of this 'Shifter plot' then I will be able to take that to Archon Jeremiah with you, and we can stop him from firebombing half of his city. What do you say?"

"I, uh, well. Do I have a choice?" Tay asked meekly.

"That's my girl. I knew a tough little cookie like you would understand. Now, my people will already have briefed Jackson, and he will give you refuge for the night, but, then, tomorrow night, you'll have to go about your work. You have until the night after that, two nights from now, to return to me with comprehensive evidence of this Shifter plot. It will take me that long to convene a meeting of the Archons anyway, so it gives you something to work towards, doesn't it?" The lady smiled her crystal-cold smile, and clapped her silk-gloved hands.

I cannot believe that she is doing this to me. I cannot believe that I ever listened to Jackson and allowed him to bring me here in the first place! Tay found herself thinking as she slowly stood up from the couch, and the room once more started to fill with the elaborate Elder peers of Manhattan society.

Gatsby tipped a wink to her over his own martini glass as he strode in, and behind her she could hear titterings of laughter.

Tay was washed by the flood of music and lights from the show outside the booth, and the velvet curtain was once again pulled down behind her.

"You," she said as Jackson sheepishly walked up to her, his purple suit glinting and catching the light of the chandeliers high above. "You knew she would use me and throw me out. You knew that she wouldn't restore me!" Tay almost shouted, jabbing Jackson in the chest angrily.

"Hey! Keep your voice down!" Jackson hissed, looking around at the other vampires nearby.

"I will not!" Tay spat the words again. "She had already decided what was to happen, and you must have known! I thought that you were my friend!"

"I *am*, Tay, I am. It's just – you wouldn't last a night out there without talking to the Archon. You're not in your district. You have no brood, no Blood Bars to rely on. You know that, Tay."

I thought I had you, Jackson, Tay thought, but the utter futility of it all stopped her from saying it. "Look – just take me back to whatever hole you call a sanctuary. Let me rest," she murmured.

"That's the spirit!" Jackson said, his tone cheery but his mannerisms nervous. "Sunrise isn't far now. A good rest and then a fresh start tomorrow night, huh!"

"I guess so." Tay was miserable as she followed the only person that she knew in all of Manhattan, and the person who had managed to completely betray her.

9. Tests

"For the sorts of vampires that cannot fit into the predatory society, to them they must be outcast. They must become feral, they must be wild. No succour will be granted to them from any Archon, and they must feed as they will; in the plains and desolate places."

- The Rule of Archons, Eleventh Mandate.

"Sire?" Matthias, now the chief of Archon Jeremiah's staff, coughed politely from where he stood at the edge of the arched doorway.

Archon Jeremiah sat in what he affectionately liked to call his 'throne room' – something his now-chief servitor Matthias honestly found a touch embarrassing. Not that he would ever have say to his Archon's face. *Or silently, for that matter,* he thought, wondering if the old rumours were true and that the oldest of Archons could indeed read people's thoughts.

Jeremiah's 'throne room' consisted of a large regency mahogany desk that had cost the Archon more than a few hundred thousand pounds, and a large, re-built Regency-era chair with gilt edgings and brass embosses. It was another part of the young Elder's careful devotion to the past and creation of an aura of mystique for himself.

The room was wood-panelled, with a tall drinks cabinet, and a small library of books. The open laptop on the ancient desk in front of the Archon was the only element that looked completely out of place in the room, and Matthias had that disturbing sensation that he always had when he walked into this room, of going back in time.

"What is it?" Jeremiah looked up, pushing his long hair back from his temples.

"The Ferals, sire, the ones that you wanted." Matthias felt a shiver of disgust go through him as he said the words. Even though he was only a lowly servitor, a mortal, he still had hopes of one day being asked to become an Elder, and so he harboured much of the same prejudices as many other of the fully-blooded vampires.

"Outstanding." Jeremiah was already in the process of standing up, his form moving in a lithe, uncoiling way that reminded the human a little of the way that a snake or a cat moved. He had that same glitter in his eyes as well, an edge of cruel excitement that Matthias had seen many times before.

Not for the first time, Matthias wondered if there was anything else that he should consider doing over the next few hours. He knew that he didn't want to watch whatever was to come.

"I trust that capturing them was no great trouble, was it?" Jeremiah had the good graces to ask as he closed the laptop and strode past the Servitor to the containment pens.

"We lost a couple of guards, sire. This pack was pretty hungry. We found them down under the old bridge, where apparently they were forming broods by the sewer outlets down there." Matthias swallowed nervously. He had seen the footage from the guards' helmet cameras as they descended into the tunnels with their UV-imitating lights. The shrieks, the flashing teeth in the dark, the mess.

"Well, good. Good. Make sure they receive some kind of medal or something," Jeremiah said off-handedly, not really listening at all to the cost of his schemes.

He strode down the corridors of his underground sanctuary, not even acknowledging the few white-suited servitors who immediately dropped to their knees as soon as he passed. Matthias hurried behind him, accepting urgent reports from the stalled servitors, and promising to notify the Archon of their importance at a more opportune time.

"Sire!" One of the white-suited mortals rushed around a corner. Matthias could see immediately that this one was young, and probably hadn't been working here at the sanctuary of Brooklyn for very long.

"Servitor!" Matthias hissed, trying to distract him, but the young man with glasses and slicked hair didn't pay any attention. He walked up to the Archon with a clipboard of reports in his hands.

"Sire? May I have a moment of your time? There are these reports that I think you need to see," the young man said.

"Oh, I need to see those, do I?" Jeremiah said, his tone friendly and cheery, but Matthias could detect the cat-playing-with-a-mouse cruelty that was barely under the surface.

The young servitor grinned, flustered. "Yes, of course; I wouldn't bother you otherwise."

"How very considerate of you; not bothering me, I mean," Jeremiah purred, and in the light of the praise the new servitor practically beamed.

"Well, thank you, sire, thank you. Well – these are complaints and missives from the mortals' councils of Brooklyn – they've been filing them all day about the market action. You know, trying to raise a bit of a stink, I guess."

"Complaints, is it?" Jeremiah feigned shock. "From the mortals?"

There was a flicker of unease across the young man's face, as if his back brain was only just catching up with what the rest of his mouth was saying, and was appalled.

"Uh, well, there have been some pickets around the market site, some chanting and protests. And, er – I thought that you may like to know the number of people who were – were..." the servitor stammered to a halt under the unblinking gaze of the Archon.

"*Restless*? Was that the word that you were looking for, my young man?" the Archon said. "You were about to tell me that the mortals are getting restless, were you not? To warn me?"

The servitor gulped, sweat appearing on his brow.

Oh no, Matthias thought, looking aside from what he knew was about to inevitably happen.

"I – uh – I thought that you would want to know, sire..." the man managed to stammer.

"Oh, you took it upon yourself to care to know what I would think. How *very* forward-thinking of you," Jeremiah sneered, and his frame seemed to start to grow, his shoulders filling out as he tensed. "Where would I be without people *warning* me about the decisions that I have made? Where would I be with all of these *mortals* getting *restless* because they are *upset* at what their sovereign chooses to do?" His words grew sharper and sharper, with a snap and a crunch implied.

The fool servitor was even stupid enough to attempt an answer. "I – uh, I don't know, sire..."

"No! You don't!" Jeremiah's hand, now morphed into a collection of iron-hard talons, burst forward, grabbing the man around the neck, causing him to sputter and choke. "*You* do not know my will, because *you* are mortal. How dare you come to me with this? How dare you question my actions?"

With each sentence, the Archon tightened his grip a little more, and gave the human a little, playful shake. Within seconds, the white-suited man had his own hands up to the Archon's singular one, and his face was gasping and going red.

"How dare you pester me with this, when I haven't asked you?" Another, more violent shake. "And how dare you (shake) come into my presence (shake) *not* on your knees!!" The final shake was the strongest, and Matthias, even though he wasn't looking, could imagine the bulging eyes and the waggling tongue as there was an audible snap and a gurgle.

With barely a sigh, Jeremiah dropped the body of the dead servitor to one side, calmly stepping over the reports, and carried on. Matthias made a quick call, telling someone that there was a clean-up in corridor 24b that needed immediate attention.

"Oh, and Matthias?" Jeremiah's voice floated back to his servant.

"Yes, sire?" he said quickly.

"While you're talking to the admin, tell them to rustle up a squad of servitor enforcers and go put an end to these rallies or pickets or whatever. I don't need to hear about it again. No containment, just straight to the Blood Banks with them all."

"As you wish, sire." Matthias relayed the orders, carefully not thinking or feeling anything. 'Straight to the Blood Banks' was his master's code for 'make sure that any troublemakers are drained dry, and their bodies disposed of'.

Chief Matthias made the necessary orders as he followed Jeremiah, speaking in calm, clipped tones into his personal mic.

The containment cells were where lesser punishments were generally meted out to Elders or even the occasional Servitor that was of exceptional value to the dark kindred. Since the Archon Jeremiah had come into power, they had been modernized and expanding, now numbering a few hundred cells comprised of nine-feet diameter 'tubes' of metal. Small hatchways could be opened in the iron doors, and through them the incarcerated could be observed, and some of them were even chained to the walls of their 'tubes'.

While intensely effective at isolating any prisoners, the containment cells were also especially designed to house Elders, those that required holding by the state rather than merely being denounced as Feral and left to starve or wander the streets (usually to a swift and gruesome end as they got hungrier and weaker). Servitors, on the other hand, were not generally given such high security – Archon Jeremiah preferring to merely kill them as 'there were plenty more where they came from'.

Elders were different. They required extra levels of incarceration, the most devious of which were the sun-filters installed at the heads of the tubes. These were, in actual fact, just adjustable flattened rods of iron and steel built across the small hatch many hundreds of feet upwards, where the tubes emerged into an old industrial yard beyond.

These bars were spaced at such a height from the tube floor that, by merely turning them, they could either lock completely and throw the inmate below into darkness during the day (and allow an Elder their natural period of rest) or they could be opened a few millimetres, forming a grate that allowed a diffuse twilight down into the tube. This had the same effect as differing strengths of UV light on an Elder, and the filters could swivel to let in bright rays of light or anywhere in between.

The cruelty of the invention was that each Elder could be matched to an appropriate level of torture. The older the Elder, the more susceptible they were to the UV rays. If the incarcerated vampire had been co-operative, then the filters could be permanently closed, allowing a degree of 'natural' life. If, however, as in the case of the Ferals inside, the Elders were maddened and enraged, then they could be kept at a half-open state, making the vampire permanently weak and ill.

The Archon Jeremiah was wildly pleased with them, and in his opinion never got to use them enough.

"Here, sire." Matthias pointed to the row of iron doors that stood next to the steel gantry on the containment block, looking for all the world more suited to a submarine than underground.

"Excellent." Jeremiah walked up to the first row of doors, where a number of white-coated servitors were already kneeling down and awaiting his nod to resume their duties. They allowed their master to step before them and look through the opened grill to the Feral vampire inside.

This one looked to be some kind of Punk in his former life. He still had on his leather jacket, but one whole sleeve was torn off and half of the lining was falling out. His jeans were in a similarly scratched and torn state, with dark stains across them that could only be dried blood.

The Feral's hair was matted and dishevelled, looking as though it might once have been dyed a shade of interesting colours, but long since washed out or obscured. Its skin was pale even by vampire standards, and looked stretched and emaciated.

Suddenly, the thing hissed and shook, looking up at the grate through which Jeremiah was peering. It sniffed the air, and saliva dripped from its pronounced teeth. It couldn't retract them anymore, nor transmogrify its claws back into fingers. Where the creature's eyes should have been, every semblance of flesh and skin had sunken away, and instead there were deep pits under pronounced brows. The darkness of predatory orbs glittered in their midst.

It shuffled, its limbs spasming and making futile clawing gestures at the walls, the air, and even itself.

"You have the next dose?" Jeremiah stepped back from the grate, and nodded for the servitors to continue.

The two stepped up, carrying between them an odd-looking rifle, which they propped through the bars of the window. Most of its barrel was shiny steel, but where the ammunition would be, there was instead a pronounced, large set of steel cylinders, one of which whirred as it kept turning the solution inside the containment system.

"Fire when ready," Jeremiah said, and settled back to wait for the outcome.

The two white-suited servitors took their time, lining up their shot, and waiting for the Punk Feral within to calm down a little before firing.

PHOOM! The noise that the medical rifle made wasn't like any other weapon; it was more like the sound of an echo in a small space. The recoil was enough that one of the two servitors staggered back, and then they hurriedly lifted the medical rifle out of the way to allow Jeremiah to observe the results.

There was a screaming and scrabbling sound from inside. The Feral had been hit in the heart, and was scrabbling at his chest, where the off-white of his blood-stained tee-shirt was stapled to his heart by a large injection-needle-shaped capsule. Within a few seconds he had hit it with enough force to snap whatever bit of metal needle was stuck in him, and was thrashing on the floor.

The Feral howled, frothing at the mouth, and, for a moment, Jeremiah couldn't be sure if that was from the pain of the shot or from the serum that had been introduced to its system. The Archon's eyes tracked the contorted movements of pain, as if they were a geography that he had yet to understand.

Slowly however, the Punk Feral within started to gasp and to pant, calming down in its passions except for the odd spasm and jerk. It lay on the bottom of its cell, its eyes dark as it stared up at the ceiling.

"Is the thing still alive?" Jeremiah asked thoughtfully.

"We could try the next stage, sire," one of the two Servitors said, and the Archon nodded.

Matthias didn't want to see or hear what might happen next – but he knew that it would be unavoidable. He would hear their screams just as he heard the screams of all of the mortals in the Security Centre the day that his Archon had decided to have his entire crew slaughtered.

The servitor who had talked went to the edge of the gantry, back from the door, and pressed a few large buttons on a small control unit there, all built into riveted steel and adding to the industrial-warehouse, submarine ambience.

There was the sound of rotating gears and the hiss of pistons far above, somewhere beyond the ceiling of their dark vault.

Jeremiah, his eyes and face shaded by the way that the grate was angled, stood, looking in at the barely-moving Feral they had recently shot.

Slowly, the light in the room started to change. It started to lighten. The Archon felt that same familiar feeling of fear and trepidation as his vampiric self-registered what this meant.

The light started to brighten, until it reached the murky glow of twilight.

Jeremiah watched the Feral blink rapidly, its eyes starting to bleed tears of blood, but otherwise, it didn't moan or whimper or call out.

"Maybe it is too past the point of sensibility to know pain," Jeremiah considered again, speaking aloud for his audience of mortals. None of them answered him.

"More," he intoned.

The twilight started to lift, filtering brighter, until the inside of the containment tube started to shine with bright detail. Jeremiah could make out every bolt and rivet in the walls, every fleck of dirt and blood that the Feral had brought in with it.

"Hghnnr!" the Feral moaned, spitting and hissing at the light that fell onto its face. It feebly lifted a claw to try to scratch out the sun.

"Damn," Jeremiah sighed. "The creature clearly feels discomfort, at the very least. More."

The light grew brighter, the Feral inside started to whimper, its wildly gesticulating hands starting to thrash more wildly. The Archon saw a change starting to come over the creature's skin. It started to darken and become blotchy. The vampire panted and attempted to roll over, but was so weak that it couldn't.

The light filtering into the tube was very bright now – as bright as a midday sun in high summer – even with the solar programme in place. The next stage would be the worse.

"More," Jeremiah said again, his voice distant as he considered what he was seeing.

The only disadvantage of the solar programme – of filling the sky above the cities with a steady stream of smog to cloud the air and change the very atmosphere – was that it made these containment cells much less efficient.

That is why Archon Jeremiah had made one little addition: he had ordered that mirrors and reflectors be added to the torture device.

The servitor at the stand pulled a lever by the side, and there was a clanking noise from somewhere high above as polished mirrors and channels were opened for the light to flow down polished reflector-tubes, before falling back into the tube below.

The light started to get uncomfortably bright, and Jeremiah, even in his shadowed space, had to start blinking away the tears of blood from his eyes. The tube was so bright that, strangely, the room started to lose details and focus. The sharpness and contrast that the vampire had seen was now replaced by glaring after-images and reflected glows. Yellows, gleaming whites, blues. Every surface that could reflect – every nut, bolt, metal wall, or the Feral's belt buckle was transformed into a glowing, incandescent star of amorphous light.

Jeremiah felt his teeth slide forward into a hiss as the vampire within fought to get out, to run away, to attack its natural enemy.

The effect on the Feral was too much. It began to writhe and keen, howl like a wild beast, unable to do anything else. Jeremiah smelled burning.

"*Agh!*" the Archon staggered back, hissing at the door.

"Shut it down!" Matthias ordered the servitor, who threw the lever and hit the buttons, killing the light as it flooded downwards into the tube instantly. Everyone standing blinked back white and orange after-images from the shards of light that had sought to escape the grilled bars of the cell.

When they could all see again, there was a toxic, greasy smell of burning that filled the air, and made Matthias gag.

"Ah well." Jeremiah peered into the containment cell and grimaced at whatever terrible sight he saw inside. "We'll have to tell the scientists to keep working on it; the serum clearly doesn't work."

"Yes, sire, as you wish." Matthias bowed his head, and followed quietly behind him, making notes, as he always did these days.

Behind them, the two scientist-servitors who had been operating the procedure returned to their own clipboards and made hurried notes.

"Test Subject 7. Introduction of synthesized Shifter-Lych blood virus. Result: Fatality, unable to resist sunlight. Prolonged hardiness to twilight and low-light conditions, however. Recommend: Double Dose? Prolonged exposure to Shifter-Lych virus? Stronger concentration of Shifter T-cells to Lych viral load? Subject: Male. Feral. Unknown."

Jeremiah smiled to himself as he ascended the metal gantry stairs up to the higher echelons of his sanctuary. Even though outside, far above, it was sunlight – he didn't feel his usual stinking headache at being awake in the sun. Even though his experiment had failed, he still felt buoyed by the results. *The Feral had appeared to not register twilight at all,* he thought to himself, aware of Matthias dragging his heels behind him. The Archon had taken the small scraps of Shifter-Lych virus that he had recovered from the mortal markets, and he was synthesizing more of it. Lots, lots more.

It will only be a matter of time before we got the right combination, Jeremiah thought, pleased.

10. Allies

"For this we know – the vampires have no special aversion to garlic, gold, or silver. Religious symbols have no special effect on them, and holy water, salt, or other blessings seem not to harm them at all. What we do know is that sunlight will harm them and hurt them, and bullet, blade, and decapitation will kill them. But know this! Their bodies are stronger than ours, and a minor wound will allow them to recover easily. They can withstand drowning, crushing, or any manner of hurts without dying – so long as they are kept alive with blood."

- *The Helsing Talks (BANNED)*

Tay grumbled as she staggered through the sewers of Manhattan. Even though, as a vampire, it took a lot to make her feel tired, cold, and exhausted, somehow the tunnels had managed to do it. She imagined that actually it must be Jackson's betrayal of her that was really getting her down.

He could have just escorted me to the edge of the city. He could have organised a route out. Maybe to Boston, or Washington.

Tay kicked a large carton of something she didn't want to know about out of her path, glad that at least she still had her boots on and some sensible clothes on.

And a Glock. She felt the reassuring weight of the gun in her jacket pocket, recently stolen from Jackson's sanctuary-bar. *Not that he'll ever know that it's gone, and if he ever does, what is he going to do? Come down after me?*

Tay had helped herself to the gun this evening, when the Archon Bethania's servitors had come to take her to where they wanted her to start her investigation. Jackson had made sure that she had enough to feed last night, and so tonight she felt full and rested.

Unfortunately. Tay sniffed unappreciatively. She would trade anything to have lost her sense of smell right now.

Unknown to most of the mortals of the city, the New York district of Manhattan is actually a very old district in the history of the West. The first vaudevilles, flop-houses, and roach hotels had stood on its dirty roadways when America was first being opened up, and ever since then it had been growing from strength to strength.

Over the years, the district had grown in opulence, almost ahead of the city, as its flag of decadence and hedonism. The brightest and strongest shows had been played there, and had drawn tourists and settlers from across the mortal world. Those generations of development had also meant invested development underground. The sewers.

Manhattan was one of the few places in America that had the large, brick-vaulted sewers spreading like catacombs under the city, to the river. They appeared to Tay as rounded, arched ceilings, with narrow walkways of tiles and stone, the lines broken every now and again by a rusted metal ladder leading upwards to a subway station or even the street itself.

It was night, and Tay had been taken to a large grate in an unremarked part of the city, where she had been forced down at gun-point to the tunnels below.

She needed no torch; her Elder eyes were sharp enough to see in the dark, (although she might not want see what was around her). She chose one of the tunnels where brackish, but clean, water was flowing in the large gulley to one side. *Overflow.* Tay considered. She remember being told that the entire island of Manhattan was in danger of flooding with a strong storm surge, and that it was only this extensive network of sewers that kept the ground water and grey water running in the right direction.

And kept all of us Elders safe and dry in our sanctuaries, Tay thought.

The tunnel system was roughly set out in a grid, with long, long stretches of nothing but noxious water and dirty stone. Tay kept on trudging onward, sure that the night was drawing long and that she wouldn't find anyone before her time was up.

And somehow I have to find evidence that the drug that the Shifters have a hold of is being shipped into the city? Tay wondered if she would even be able to find a Feral *capable* of rational speech, let alone friendly enough to actually aid her.

It could have been me. The thought struck her suddenly. *Still could.* She had only been a few meals away from starting to become truly Feral, not caring about her appearance or where she slept, just focusing on the next meal, and then the next and the next.

Tay hated the thought of being so close to losing control. *But isn't that we are always like, us vampires? Always only barely in control?*

Tay walked on into the darkness, beginning to lose sense of where she had come from.

I haven't turned off, have I? She was sure that Bethania's servitors had said that a pack of Ferals was sighted down here. That all she had to do was ingratiate herself to them...

Her foot hit something on the floor, and the shape skidded along the narrow pavement. Tay stopped, as the small shape smelled of blood.

Old blood. Something dead.

The vampire crept towards it, to see that it was a rat. It was dead and had died by all of its blood being drained from its body. That could only mean one thing.

Tay felt herself tense up, her senses straining to hear what might lie beyond the next bend or intersection. It was disorienting in the sewers, small sounds echoing off of the tiles for what must be miles, or the water itself having a dampening effect on sound, making far away noises seem close, and near-to noises come from far off. There was a low wailing noise, like the sound of wind moving through underground pipes.

Or was that a person moaning? Someone – or something hungry?

Tay walked on, carefully taking out her heavy Glock and making sure that it was loaded. Up ahead there was an intersection, a cross-roads, like the many others where small metal bridges spanned the waterway to allow the sewer workers (if any still came down here) to continue their work.

Rags and boxes were piled at the edge, remnants left by the homeless people who must have called this place their home. Tay wondered at the perversity of it all, the fact that above ground one of the richest cities in the world existed, whilst just a few hundred feet below, some of the poorest might be starving to death.

It's a predatory society, she reminded herself. *Blood pays for blood.*

The first detail that gave away that anything was wrong was a subtle rustling in the layers of newspapers and rags up ahead.

Tay was almost at the intersection when the rags and newspaper were swept aside, and something hissed from the depths of trash at her. She raised her gun, ready to fire at it, whatever it was, but felt something heavy and sharp score her back.

More behind me! She tumbled forward, almost into the arms of the rising Feral vampire as it leapt for her from the trash. The second, behind her, must have been almost entirely submerged in the dark waters of the sewer, floating almost to the edge of her ankles when it sprang out.

Tay rolled, ducking under the sweeping arms of the Feral ahead, feeling a line of cold fire erupt on the back of her neck as she just managed to reach the small metal bridge, and spun around.

There behind her, were two Ferals lurching toward her, momentarily disoriented by her faster reactions, but gaining speed by the millisecond. One was barely bigger than she was, wild hair matted and half-dreaded, its face a mess of teeth and a broken jaw that had healed oddly. Vampires can heal quickly, so the fact that this one looked disfigured either meant that the injury was done years before the moral turned, or that it has been so deprived of blood that it could not even maintain its own body.

The second one was even worse-looking, almost without hair and with slimy, heavy clothes stuck to its body. Its skin was pale and not as emaciated as the other one – this one looked blotchy and bloated, and Tay realized it was due to the long, long hours and days that it must spend in the water.

The true-blooded vampire started backing down the bridge, hearing it grind and squeak underneath her.

This one is so weak that it just lies in its hole of trash, and this one is so weak that it just floats, dead, in the sewers until something with fresh blood wanders close. She raised her gun.

For a moment, Tay found herself speculating if, somehow, these two monsters had participated in their own bizarre form of hunt together; whether this was their set-up, one on the pavement, the other in the water, and between them they could startle and capture any hazardous other creature. The vampire had terrifying visions of Ferals that were like the deep-sea creatures of the octopus, preying on each other and on their brethren Ferals.

No. They didn't have enough intelligence left to hunt as a co-ordinated pack.

Tay pulled the trigger, and the sound was deafening in such a small space.

BOOM! BOOM! BOOM! Tay didn't realize just how many times she was pulling the trigger until the smoke started to clear. One of the Ferals, the one which had been on the pavement, was shivering wetly on the floor, and where the other one should have been, there was nothing but a smear of gore.

Will it have stopped them? How strong are they? Tay thought wildly, and tried to calm herself down. *I mustn't get spooked. I'm worse than these creatures. They aren't even full vampires...*

Something splashed in the black water, and Tay spun, *BOOM!* Another bullet into the dark. The sewer water swallowed it whole, without even making a sound.

A flicker out of her eye on the other side of the bridge...

Tay turned, felt something grab her ankle, and she was falling; a sensation of shock as she toppled, her leg banging on the metal bridge and then the impact of the cold overflow water of the sewer... the taste of water gone wrong, or something oily and rotten.

The grip on her ankle never ceased, and it was joined by another grip on her wrist – and then another. A small, silent part of Tay's mind registered that there were more hands holding her than there had been Ferals in front of her. There were more of them in the water.

She screamed, releasing a stream of bubbles to the surface, and thrashed, kicking out to connect with something solid before her, and something underneath her.

The back of her neck was burning, and she couldn't work out if it was because of the dirty water getting into the claw mark that she already had, or perhaps it was another vampire biting her. Her brain processed in an instant, worrying in the thrashing darkness. *What if it was another vampire about to bite down on her spinal cord, already just centimetres from severing her head from her body?*

Tay felt a surge of dark, fear-borne hatred, and cavorted even wilder. One of her elbows met something firm, and felt it give way with a crunch. Her boot scraped along a stretch of tendons like coiled rope.

Tay fought and scratched like she never had before. Somewhere in the gloom she had given up her gun and had reverted to more primal, vampiric weapons: Claws, teeth, head-butts, knees.

In the midst of her frenzy, suddenly something gave way and she was exploding from the surface of the water, choking and spewing water from her lungs, hissing at the white-foam churn of the fight around her. There were other white, bloated Feral forms down there, rising to grab at her again.

Tay shouted, kicking at them, clambering for the ledge, and running into the darkness as the knot of Ferals swam and groaned after her.

Tay's footsteps sounded heavy and loud in the tunnel, even to her own ears. Every sound echoed off of the tiled walls all around, returning to her so that she was surrounded by the clattering of a million feet, a multitude, a horde.

Tay ran through the darkness, her unnatural eyes widening her pupils until she just had blackened orbs, scanning the water and the ledge ahead for any signs of another Feral attack. She didn't know for how long she had been running, or how far. When she eventually stopped, she couldn't hear the groans and hisses of the Ferals behind her, but instead she heard footsteps, and the distant rebound of her own gunshots, that sounded like thunder rumbling over the horizon.

I must have lost them, the vampire thought, *somewhere in the turns and tunnels.*

Of course, the obvious result was that she had managed to lose herself as well.

Was that a moan or a groan of approaching Ferals, or was it just the rise of wind in the tunnels? Had she actually lost her pursuers or were they merely laying a new trap for her?

There. She was certain that she had heard something then, coming from up ahead. A sound, like a polite cough. It was almost so quiet and inconsequential that Tay was about to ignore it. Another sound of the city, until she realized...

She wasn't in the city. Anyone down here with her had to be a Feral.

Tay took another step forward, in the direction that she thought the sound had come from. Was she hearing things? Had it been her imagination? Who else could be down here?

The vampire reached for her gun, then cursed under her breath when she realized that she had lost it earlier. Gone, the way of everything else, it seemed. Abandoned somewhere at the bottom of a sewer.

Looks like you'll just have to do this one alone then, Tay, she thought to herself, extending her claws as she crept forward.

The wind whistled down the tunnel towards her, a low moaning. Far behind her, she heard a distant splashing sound of the dirty waters. *Was that a growl up ahead?*

The woman's ears strained as she moved with elaborate slowness. She could feel the damp of water as it slid between her clothes and her skin. She could feel the brushes of air that were rising from the tunnels ahead. Her predatory mind raced, analysing every movement and action ahead to see if she were about to be trapped, or herded into disaster.

The Ferals are still predators, after all. In fact – that is all that they are, Tay realised. *They are like us, what I should be if someone stripped all of the human bits away, and just left the hungry vampire inside me, instead.*

There was another sound from up ahead, a scrape of something, metal or hard surface against another. Tay crouched. It seemed to be coming from a rounded service tunnel that opened out into her tunnel, above the level of the ledge. *All of these tunnels and pipes*, she thought. *All of them driven and diving and winding around and through each other, as ever more desperate populations sought to answer the problems of over-population.*

Perhaps the Archons are right, that it's almost a good thing that the Elders have culls. Tay found her fear overriding her conscience. *The mortals are almost about to collapse in on their own greed.*

Tay shook her head quickly. It didn't matter. She was overthinking, trying to not focus on the tide of monsters that might come pouring out of that tunnel at any moment. She tensed her muscles, got ready to pounce.

Click. "I wouldn't, if I were you," a voice said behind her.

How did they creep up on me? was the first thought that crossed Tay's mind, and the next, that it was a woman's voice behind her.

"Can I turn around?" Tay asked.

"Only if you do it slow enough that I won't have to blow your brains out," the woman replied, her tone sounding almost comical.

"Okay. Turning now." Tay took a slow step to turn around, and immediately a gun barrel appeared, hovering right over her temple. Behind it, the shape of a woman, smaller than Tay, of American-Chinese heritage. Her hair was a garish shade of electric red, and she wore multiple layers of rags, blankets, and mismatched clothes sewn to each other in a patchwork over her body.

Even in the near pitch-black, the woman's eyes were dark and round, and her skin pale. It was clear that she too was an Elder.

"Uh. Do you come here often?" Tay tried an attempt at humour, and the woman just scowled, subtly readjusting her grip on her pistol.

Yup, no way I can dodge it this close. Tay sighed, lowering her hands slowly.

"Look, the way I see it – you can kill me anytime you want." Tay shrugged. "If you're good enough to sneak up on me – and live down here with those…"

"Ferals?" The woman arched an eyebrow. "I'd be careful if I were you; you might insult my delicate sensibilities."

That was when the penny dropped. *"You're* a Feral too," Tay said. "But, uh, you're not like the others…"

"You mean I'm not a mindless, growling zombie?" The woman smirked wider, still keeping her gun trained on the newcomer. "Well, not *all* of us Ferals are, see?" she said pointedly. "Some of us manage to get enough to eat around here."

Tay felt a shiver of apprehension that she herself might be on the menu.

Then the stranger drew a breath and relaxed her guard, letting her arm relax and her gun sit at her hip, still pointing at Tay, but a gesture of pacification if nothing else. "Also, all of us Ferals have to start somewhere, and if you made it down here, then I would say you pretty much deserve to at least see the Collective."

"The Collective?" Tay said.

"Enough questions. You'll see. Now get up into that tunnel before I *do* decide to have a snack on my way home from work." The woman grinned cruelly. "And our neighbours will probably drift down this way soon enough, unless we're out of here."

"Your neighbours. Right. The *other* Ferals." Tay did as she was told, hoisting her wet and aching body into the dark metal tube and starting to crawl forward through the murk. "By the way, what should I call you?"

"Just Zhang," the woman replied, her voice muffled behind her as she crawled after her through the tunnel.

It took a while for even Tay's vampiric eyes to adjust to the gloom of the tunnel, but there seemed to be no danger of taking a wrong turn, as the tunnel was a solid piece of metal bored through the very concrete of the sewers. It travelled downward at a gentle slope, leaving moisture and dirt on Tay's hands and knees. Occasionally she could hear a rising moaning sound, and realized that it was air moving through the tunnel itself, creating a vast echo chamber.

They kept on crawling for what felt like hours, and Tay started to feel tired.

"It must be near dawn," Tay was saying, her voice becoming drowsier by the second.

"It is – but down here we don't pay much attention to that," Zhang said behind her. "You'll soon see that we all have our own ways of doing things down here."

I bet you do, Tay thought. "Like kidnapping strangers?" she said.

"Like making sure those strangers aren't scouts, sent to cull my friends," Zhang replied, in just as easy and light a tone as the question had been asked.

Fair enough, the vampire thought, and kept crawling.

Tay was almost asleep as she moved steadily downwards when they reached their destination point. She started to hear more noises, bangs and clanks of industry, hissing voices, a gentle roar that was growing louder and louder...

And light! There is light! Tay, for almost the first time in her life, was thankful for the light that she saw ahead of her. Her paranormal senses could tell immediately that it wasn't sunlight, by a mechanism or secret sense that she didn't even know that she possessed. It was an electric glow, resolving itself into hands, reaching into the tunnel to grab her shoulders...

"Hey!" Tay managed to shout, just as the hands pulled her out roughly, dumping her onto something soft: a pile of half-rotten cardboard and litter.

Tay snarled, rising to a crouch to look around, wondering if in fact Zhang had been lying, and she was about to become somebody's lunch.

And then she stopped snarling when she saw just what was around her.

It was a community.

In what must have once been an underground pumping station of some kind – whose enclosed engines still roared and whined from their rusted-over massive cylinders – each bigger than a car, the Ferals had managed to build a sort of shanty town.

There were pallets and old bits of wood holding up tents and stretches of canvas. There were small cleared areas that obviously served as a meeting place: a large round depression in the room where the arrangement of pipes roughly formed a series of steps. Vampires, in general, do not need a lot of the things that mortals require, just comfort, a place to rest, and a place to feed. Some vampires cling to their belongings over the years, making grander and grander sanctuaries fit for princes and millionaires, but many others prefer a minimalist lifestyle. These Ferals, it would seem, were more like the latter than the former. They required only warm, dry places to rest, and places to refrigerate and keep blood. Tay could see banks of jury-rigged refrigeration units stacked up like banks of amplifiers, wires and pipes thrumming between them.

But what struck Tay the most about the Ferals around her was not *how* they lived, but that they lived here at all. She looked around at a host of vampiric faces, some old, some young, some hopeless and wary, but all apparently peaceful.

Tay opened and closed her mouth, unsure of what to say. Everything that she had been told (and had already seen) down here led her to believe that the Ferals were a cruel and terrible scourge of society. That they were barely civilized, beasts and monsters, like the ones that she faced higher in the tunnels.

These looked at her with a wary sort of generosity, with intelligence clear in their eyes. There must have been easily nearly a couple of hundred Elders living cheek by jowl down here – more than Tay had ever seen in one place at one time.

"Not what you were expecting, is it?" Zhang said, dropping down beside her. She was immediately met by a resounding chorus of cheers and greetings.

"Rat-mother!"

"Rat-mother saves all!" they said.

Tay looked askance at Zhang, who threw her brood a sarcastic look. "Enough of that, enough."

"*Rat-mother?*" Tay asked.

"It's their joke. Every time I go out hunting, I come back with rats, and they think that I must be farming them up there or something." Zhang made a calming, waving gesture with her hands at the crowd.

"Everyone? Listen up – we've got a new addition, it seems. This lady faced off the ghouls at the top, and managed to make her way almost all the way down here to us before I caught up with her. She did have a gun, but she went and lost that."

There was a chorus of groans from around them. Guns must be in short supply down here, a few considering looks at the toughness of the Elder who had managed to make it through the hordes of deranged Ferals above. None of them were licking their lips as though about to devour her.

"Those – uh, those *ghouls*. They are the Ferals that couldn't feed?" Tay asked.

"That, or couldn't handle life down here. We get wanderers every now and again; like yourself, people have been kicked out of the Archon's society above. They eventually filter down through the city to make their way to here, and if they make it through the ghouls – then, well, they get welcomed," Zhang replied. "Some of them are beyond helping, though, and more than half-ghoulish already." The rat-mother shrugged. "We do what we can, and leave the ones that we can't help."

Tay shuddered at the thought of being left up there if she hadn't passed whatever mysterious benchmark that Zhang must use to assess potential applicants to her Feral collective.

"And your name?" Zhang asked.

"Tay," the vampire said. "Tay Maslov, lately of Brooklyn."

"You're a long way from Brooklyn, Tay Maslov," Rat-mother Zhang said sharply. "Come, we'll get you some food. Clear off." She batted her hand at some of the onlookers, and gradually the crowd of Ferals started to disperse.

"Excuse me, excuse me..." a thin man with the tattoo of a skull over his face reached to pull at Tay's still-sodden sleeve. Tay reacted instinctively, pulling away and hissing. *I guess I'm still a little jumpy from the attack earlier.* As soon as she saw his face, however, with its look of hurt, she felt instantly sorry.

"I'm sorry, I just – it's been a while," Tay said.

"Don't crowd her, Damien!" Zhang hissed at the Elder, who looked barely older than his early twenties.

"I'm sorry, sorry, it's just – you come from Brooklyn? Do you know Angola Heights? There was a sanctuary over there of Elders, Leilani, Bubokov, Azi..." he asked in his thick Eastern European accent.

Tay shook her head. "I'm sorry, Damien; I don't know. It's been a while since I've been in Archon Jeremiah's good graces enough to know what's happening in his district," she said, although she remembered hearing that there was a brood from Angola Heights that had been brought in by Jeremiah for 'unpatriotic activity' – whatever *that* meant these days. She didn't tell him.

"Oh, okay, thanks anyway." The young-looking Elder fell backwards, and Zhang hurried Tay onward, towards where a makeshift awning was set up next to the refrigeration units.

"Here. You'll need this," she said as soon as they ducked inside the awning to find a cool, dark area with long benches running up and down the middle of the aisle. The shapes of other Elders sat huddled in the gloom, and it gave Tay a warm, almost womb-like experience. Nothing like the sterile, carefully measured and accounted for bureaucracy of the Blood Banks on the surface.

"We've been trying out different things down here, since we started. Different ways of doing things," Zhang explained, disappearing for a moment to the back of the units, and coming back with a sterile metal canister filled with blood; one for her, and one for Tay. "The Blood Bank idea is the first to go. It makes the transaction of blood clinical, non-personal. And all of us Elders know that *dreaming* is nothing but personal, right?"

Tay nodded, unsure whether she wanted to indulge in front of the leader of this underground community, but saw that she was already starting herself.

"Where do you get all of this blood?" Tay asked lightly as she unscrewed the pressurized top, smelling it appreciatively.

Zhang shot her a look. "We have our contacts. Allies on the surface."

I wonder who? Tay thought as she tipped the canister back, drank, and *dreamed*.

THE END
HERE ENDS BOOK 1: *THE LOST VAMPIRE*. MAKE SURE YOU FOLLOW TAY & KAIDEN'S DARK ADVENTURES IN BOOK 2: *THE COST OF BLOOD*.

COST OF BLOOD:
Fleeing the Archon Jeremiah's rage and his purge of Brooklyn, the vampire Tay Maslov has sought aid from neighbouring Archon Bethania of Manhattan, decadent, nihilistic Bethania. The forever-young makes a deal with the young Feral; be her spy and all will be well. Perhaps she will even regain her place at an Archon's unholy side. But with the Shadow War between the Shifters and the Elders heating up, Kaiden and Tay find themselves dragged into a twisting game of play and counter-play, as the different factions threaten to tear the city apart...

NOTE: Free Excerpt of Victoria – Daughter of Darkness included at end of book!

BIT-LIT SERIES
BEST SELLING AUTHOR
W.J. MAY
LOST VAMPIRE
W.J. MAY
COST OF BLOOD
W.J. MAY
PRICE OF DEATH
W.J. MAY

Bit Lit Series:

Lost Vampire - Book 1
Cost of Blood – Book 2
NOW AVAILABLE
Book 3
Coming January 2016

Note from the Author;

I hope you enjoyed reading Lost Vampire. I'm so excited to continue this series!

If you have a moment to post a review to let others know about the story, I would greatly appreciate it! I love hearing from my fans so feel free to send me a message on Facebook or by email so we can chat.

\
All the best, W.J. May

W.J. May Info:

Website: http://www.wanitamay.yolasite.com
Facebook: https://www.facebook.com/pages/Author-WJ-May-FAN-PAGE/141170442608149
SIGN UP FOR **W.J. May's Newsletter** to find out about new releases, updates, cover reveals and even freebies!
http://eepurl.com/97aYf

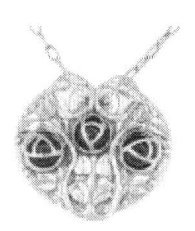

More from W.J. May

THE CHRONICLES OF KERRIGAN

Rae of Hope is FREE!
Book Trailer:
http://www.youtube.com/watch?v=gILAwXxx8MU

BOOK BLURB:

How hard do you have to shake the family tree to find the truth about the past?

Fifteen year-old Rae Kerrigan never really knew her family's history. Her mother and father died when she was young and it is only when she accepts a scholarship to the prestigious Guilder Boarding School in England that a mysterious family secret is revealed.

Will the sins of the father be the sins of the daughter?

As Rae struggles with new friends, a new school and a star-struck forbidden love, she must also face the ultimate challenge: receive a tattoo on her sixteenth birthday with specific powers that may bind her to an unspeakable darkness. It's up to Rae to undo the dark evil in her family's past and have a ray of hope for her future.

Hidden Secrets Saga:
Download Seventh Mark part 1 For FREE
Book Trailer:
http://www.youtube.com/watch?v=Y-_vVYC1gvo

RADIUM HALOS – THE SENSELESS SERIES
Book 1 is FREE:

Book Blurb:

Everyone needs to be a hero at one point in their life.

The small town of Elliot Lake will never be the same again.

Caught in a sudden thunderstorm, Zoe, a high school senior from Elliot Lake, and five of her friends take shelter in an abandoned uranium mine. Over the next few days, Zoe's hearing sharpens drastically, beyond what any normal human being can detect. She tells her friends, only to learn that four others have an increased sense as well. Only Kieran, the new boy from Scotland, isn't affected.

Fashioning themselves into superheroes, the group tries to stop the strange occurrences happening in their little town. Muggings, break-ins, disappearances, and murder begin to hit too close to home. It leads the team to think someone knows about their secret – someone who wants them all dead.

An incredulous group of heroes. A traitor in the midst. Some dreams are written in blood.

Courage Runs Red
Book Blurb:

What if courage was your only option?

When Kallie lands a college interview with the city's new hot-shot police officer, she has no idea everything in her life is about to change. The detective is young, handsome and seems to have an unnatural ability to stop the increasing local crime rate. Detective Liam's particular interest in Kallie sends her heart and head stumbling over each other.

When a raging blood feud between vampires spills into her home, Kallie gets caught in the middle. Torn between love and family loyalty she must find the courage to fight what she fears the most and possibly risk everything, even if it means dying for those she loves.

Victoria: Daughter of Darkness
Book 1 is Free
Description:

Only Death Could Stop Her Now

The Daughters of Darkness is a series of female heroines who may or may not know each other, but all have the same father, Vlad Montour.

Victoria is a Hunter Vampire, one of the last of her kind. She's the best of the best.

When she finds out one of her marks is actually her sister she lets her go, only to end up on the wrong side of the council.

Forced to prove herself she hunts her next mark, a werewolf. Injured and hungry, she is forced to do what she must to survive. Her actions upset the ancient council and she finds herself now being the one thing she has always despised – the Hunted.

This is Tori's story by W.J. May. This is a novella. As a courtesy, the author wishes to inform you this novella does end with a cliffhanger.

Shadow of Doubt
Part 1 is FREE!
Book Trailer:
http://www.youtube.com/watch?v=LZK09Fe7kgA

Book Blurb:
What happens when you fall for the one you are forbidden to love?

Erebus is a bit of a lost soul. He's a guy so he should be out to have fun but unlike the rest of his kind, he is solemn and withdrawn. That is, until he meets Aurora, a law student at Cornell University. His entire world is shaken. Feelings he's never had and urges he's never understood take over. These strange longings drive him to question everything about himself

When a jealous ex stalks back into his life, he must decide if he is willing to risk everything to be with Aurora. His desire for her could destroy her, or worse, erase his own existence forever.

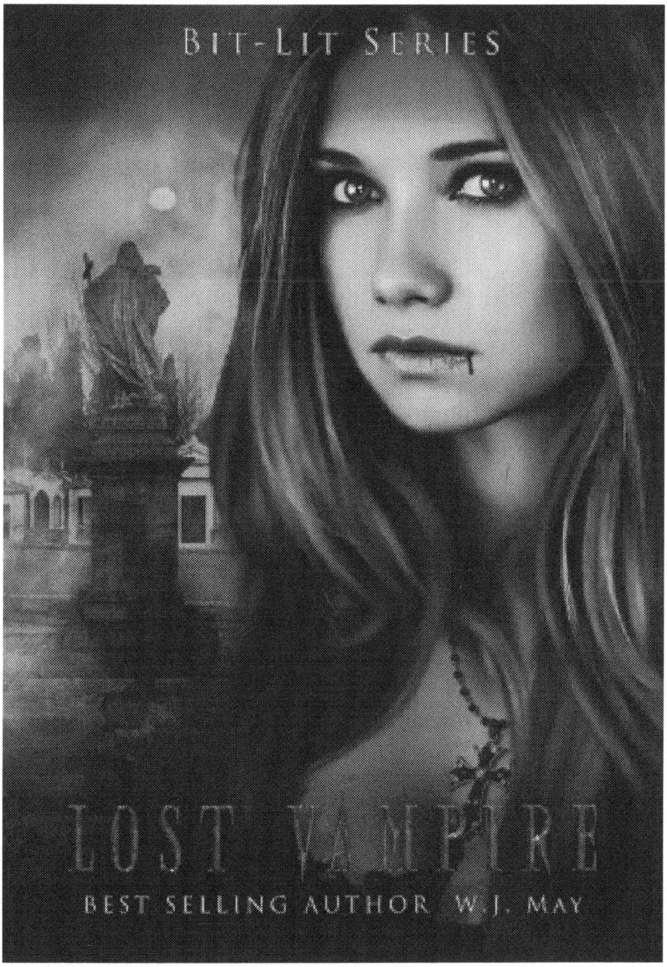
BIT-LIT SERIES
LOST VAMPIRE
BEST SELLING AUTHOR W.J. MAY

FREE EXCERPT

Daughter of Darkness
VICTORIA
Book I
By
W.J. May
Copyright 2015 by W.J. May

This e-book is licensed for your personal enjoyment only. This e-book may not be re-sold or given away to other people. If you would like to share this book with another person, please purchase an additional copy for each recipient. If you're reading this book and did not purchase it, or it was not purchased for your use only, then please return to Smashwords.com and purchase your own copy. Thank you for respecting the hard work of the author.

All rights reserved. No part of this publication may be reproduced, stored in or introduced into a retrieval system, or transmitted, in any form, or by any means (electronic, mechanical, photocopying, recording, or otherwise) without the prior written permission of both the copyright owner and the above publisher of this book.

This is a work of fiction. Names, characters, places, brands, media, and incidents are either the product of the author's imagination or are used fictitiously. Any resemblance to actual person, living or dead, events, or locales is entirely coincidental. The author acknowledges the trademarked status and trademark owners of various products referenced in this work of fiction, which have been used without permission. The publication/use of these trademarks is not authorized, associated with, or sponsored by the trademark owners.

All rights reserved.
Copyright 2015 by W.J. May
Cover design by: Book Cover by Design
Edited by: PBYP

No part of this book may be used or reproduced in any manner whatsoever without written permission, except in the case of brief quotations embodied in articles and reviews.

4 authors will each take a different daughter born from the Prince of Darkness, Vlad Montour. (Also known as Vlad the Impaler, an evil villain from history)

Blair – Chrissy Peebles
Jezebel – Kristen Middleton
Victoria – W.J. May
Lotus – C.J. Pinard

W.J. MAY

Victoria, Book 1 by W.J. May
Huntress, Book II by W.J. May
Coveted, Book III by W.J. May
Blair, by Chrissy Peebles

Blair is half witch and half vampire. She lives with a coven of witches and hasn't had any contact with her vampire heritage. Blair is living the perfect life until one day, everything crashes down around her. She is forced to leave everything she knows and loves, and must go on the run to save her life.

This is Blair's story by Chrissy Peebles. This is a novella. As a courtesy, the author wishes to inform you this novella does end with a cliffhanger. The next book will continue the story.

This is an adult book series and this series does contain scenes for readers that are 18+

Victoria

Only Death Could Stop Her Now

The Daughters of Darkness is a series of female heroines who may or may not know each other, but all have the same father, Vlad Montour.

Victoria is a Hunter Vampire

Description:
Victoria
Only Death Could Stop Her Now

The Daughters of Darkness is a series of female heroines who may or may not know each other, but all have the same father, Vlad Montour.

Victoria is a Hunter Vampire, one of the last of her kind. She's the best of the best.

When she finds out one of her marks is actually her sister she let's her go, only to end up on the wrong side of the council.

Forced to prove herself she hunts her next mark, a werewolf. Injured and hungry, she is forced to do what she must to survive. Her actions upset the ancient council and she finds herself now being the one thing she has always despised—the Hunted.

This is Tori's story by W.J. May. This is a novella. As a courtesy, the author wishes to inform you this novella does end with a cliffhanger. The next book coming out in early Autumn (or sooner) will continue the story.

This is an adult book series and does contain scenes for readers that are 16+

Preface

Darkness – it's the first thing I remembered and it'll be the last thing I will ever forget.
When I changed, it was dark and cold,
Kind of like that book that starts out; "It was a dark and stormy night..."
I should have been terrified, but I didn't feel any fear. Something inside of me changed that night. Something died.

That was a very long time ago...

Chapter 1

The howling of the wind muffled another type of cry, which pierced the night air. I leaned over on the tree branch where I perched. Another scoundrel had been caught. They were getting harder to find these days. Time had caught up with the hunters. All the others had grown smarter or, more likely, run and hid. Survival of the fittest.

Vampires were the strongest species. I believed it without a doubt.

A branch snapped about forty feet away from me. I tensed and held my breath. I moved my arm to collect an arrow from behind me and nestled it into the bow. The black leather outfit I wore fit tight but snug. It made no sound, just moved like part of my body. All the hunters wore the same material. Another sound had me swinging the bow and aiming it a few feet in front of the tree I sat in.

I blinked and focussed, trying to determine if the noise maker below me might be friend or foe. Vlad preferred to kill first, then check who it was. The guy was an idiot – and also my father.

"Victoria?" Hamish called up.

I kept my arrow trained on him and glared down, knowing my sapphire blue eyes would flash against the moon's reflection. "What?" I barked.

He ducked and cowered. "Don't shoot me."

"What is it?" My hands remained in their position.

"One of the dogs found a scent. He says it's what you're looking for."

Without hesitation, I slipped from the branch and fell the fifty feet. Midway down, I released the arrow still trained on Hamish. I landed like a cat, perfectly on my feet, and threw my head back to toss my jet-black hair over my shoulders.

Hamish jumped and squealed. His reflexes were fast for a human, weak for a half vampire. He annoyed me, but he was loyal. One of the few I trusted. "You almost got me!" He touched his ear and swore. "You nicked my ear! I'm bleeding."

I smelled the blood before he noticed it. I could feel my eyes burn and knew they would be a bright sky blue now. The human part of him still smelled toxic. I blinked and ignored the burning in my throat. "You're fine." I tucked the bow in the case behind me and pulled the gun from the holster on my hip. I pointed it behind Hamish. "He's not so good."

Some sort of Halfling or supernatural lay forever silent on the ground behind Hamish. *How the idiot never heard it...* I puffed a breath out. It didn't matter. "Where's the wolf?" I started in the direction Hamish had come, not bothering to wait for him.

He raced to catch up, hanging close on my shoulder. "It's by the water. It stinks like wet dog."

"So do you." I sped up my pace and sniffed the air. The werewolf was maybe two hundred yards away. I edged my way close to the stream and leaped across. Hamish tried to copy and landed halfway in the water.

Malcolm, my hunting partner, stood leaning against a tree waiting for me. He pointed to the black and gray wolf by the water. "Finally!" He pushed away from the bark and came to stand by the wolf.

The wolf lifted its massive head and watched me with its amber eyes. He had to be nearly ninety now. I'd had him since he was a pup. I rubbed his right ear, near the missing chunk of fur and skin. "What did you find, sweetie?"

Malcolm snorted. "You talk nicer to the bag of fleas than anyone else."

I ignored him and grinned when Eddie growled from deep in his throat. "Don't piss him off again, Malcolm."

Eddie backed away from my hand and moved around the large oak tree Malcolm had been leaning against. He came around the other side in human form. "The scent disappeared here at the water, I think she's traveling in it to hide from us."

"She? Are you sure?" It had to be the one we wanted.

Eddie nodded, his shaggy hair shaking in agreement. "Positive."

I looked at Malcolm, who seemed as surprised as me. "Can you tell which way she went?"

Eddie pointed west. "I think this way. The current pulls the scent down so I'm guessing she went against it to try and throw you off."

I hitched my gun back in its holster. "Then let's go. It'll be daylight in a couple of hours and we're going to need to find somewhere to go underground or out of sunlight. I don't want her getting any more of a head start than she's already got. She'll be dead either tonight or tomorrow. Preferably this evening."

"I don't know if she's alone," Eddie said quietly. He hunched down, uncomfortable in human form. He spent most of his time as a wolf now, and usually by my side.

"She's got a posse?"

He shook his head. "I don't know."

I froze and sniffed the air. "I smell blood."

Malcolm and Hamish stopped behind me. "Lots of it," Malcolm added.

"Oh shit." I started running. "It's already begun."

"What has?" Malcolm kept up easily with my pace. Beside him, Eddie turned back to wolf form.

I had no idea where Hamish was. He'd catch up eventually. It annoyed me I had to take him along. Three was not company. My dog didn't count. "We're hunting a witch. Or half witch, she's not turned yet. The massive blood scent makes me think someone else wants her turned."

"Or wants her dead more than we do." Malcolm squinted across the dark sky.

Moments later I grabbed his jacket to hold him back. "Shhh!" I hissed, my incisors extending in excitement. "I hear her. She's nearby. Listen to her heart."

I held my finger to my lips and pointed to the left. I moved toward the right, Eddie close on my heels. One of his paws caught on a branch. It snapped, cutting the crickets and insects of the nights' songs.

"Who's there?" a soft, unsure voice called out.

The crickets resumed their chirping.

A gust of wind picked up and blew my hair into my face. Annoyed, I pushed it behind my ear. I edged my way to the heartbeat and motioned for Malcolm to come around the rear. He nodded. I crept through the foliage and stepped clear in front of it.

A beautiful girl, looking about the same age as me, stood panting about twenty feet away. Dark hair, light, smooth skin. She had the potential to be beautiful, she just didn't know it yet. The age thing might be deceiving though, I looked twenty, but had been born too long to remember when. I stared at her eyes; they had a purple hue. "You think you're royalty or something?"

Her hand clutched near her heart. She was scared, but strangely, she also seemed angry.

"Looks like a lot of people want you dead." I glanced down at her blood-splattered clothes. "Me, included."

The girl swallowed hard, her pulse thrusting against the artery in her neck. I licked my lips and felt the burning in my eyes as they changed. I held my breath, not wanting the scent of blood in my nostrils. It would only entice me.

Her lips trembled. "I was just living this normal life, and suddenly everyone wants to kill me."

"I'm only interested in doing my job."

"Please let me go," she begged.

Seriously? Why did people still ask these days? "I can't do that." I shrugged. "You have something my boss wants."

She snorted. "Yeah, my powers." She paused, as if trying to think of a way to stall the inevitable. "What's your name?"

I stared up at the sky then back at her. "Really? At this point, does it matter?"

She straightened, her hands going to her hips. "I deserve to know the name of my executioner."

"Back in King Henry's time, the job was held in high regard. Nobody knew the executioners. They were revered and feared."

The crazy girl held her ground. I could almost hear Malcolm chuckling behind her.

"Tori. Think of me as a supernatural bounty hunter. Unfortunately for you, you're my target. I don't make the hit list. I just do what I'm told. We all have a job. It's nothing personal." My eyes burned again as my incisors pressed against the flesh behind my lips. I ran my tongue over them, their points sharp and familiar.

She shook her head. "You smell like a vampire. I can't believe you'd kill your own kind. How sick and twisted is that?"

"Twisted is my middle name." I glanced at Malcolm behind her. Did he know she was a half vamp? That wasn't in her file. I pulled both guns from the holsters on my hips and pointed them at her. I'd had enough of this conversation.

The girl sucked in a sharp breath and her hands began to glow.

"Shit!" I crouched, ready to spring at her or away – whatever move was necessary. "Her magic's been activated."

Malcolm raced to my side, glaring at the girl. "When?"

I gripped my weapon tighter. "I've no idea."

He moved closer so our shoulders touched. "We should've been told about this." He pulled the gun from his belt out.

"This changes everything."

"She doesn't know how to use it. She's a baby wizard with nobody to guide her."

"Looks like she's doing a good job to me."

"She's winging it!

The glow in her hands turned into a ball of fire. "She's dangerous!"

Malcolm stepped toward her. "She won't kill us. I've studied her case file. She's got way too many morals. She's a nurse and lives to save people, not hurt them."

What was Malcolm thinking? You back any animal into a corner and they're going to come out fighting, especially if the weapon's aimed at them.

"Just let me go." The girl stared directly at me.

I raised both guns and aimed them at her, daring her to move.

Her hands glimmered stronger, glowing with energy. Red balls of light centered in the palms of her hands, some kind of sparkling electricity. Screw fireballs. This was some sort of sun ray, or something vampires couldn't deflect.

Eddie growled at my side, ready to defend me, even if it meant his own death. When the girl moved, he lunged at her. She threw crackling balls of fire at him. Dirt and leaves exploded all around us like grenades on a battlefield.

"What happened to those high morals of hers?" I snapped at Malcolm as I scrambled to my feet.

"Oops. I thought I had her pegged."

Oops? He nearly got us and my dog killed!

The girl sprang into the overgrowth and sped off.

I wiped the mud off my face and straightened. "I'm going to kill that bitch."

Chapter 2

"What's the girl's name?"

"Blair something."

I glared at Malcolm as we walked in the direction the girl, Blair, had taken off in. "Eddie!" I called out. "Find her scent. Hundred bucks says she's back in the stream. On purpose this time."

Hamish came crashing through the forest, arms floundering as he tried to avoid the brush and branches hitting his face. "What'd I miss?" He glanced around. "Where's the mark?"

"Running like a scared rabbit." Malcolm glanced up through the trees. "We don't have much time."

"Then we'd better not let her get away a second time." I sped through the forest, following Eddie this time. We moved with supernatural speed, leaving Hamish to try and keep up again. The guy was such a casualty. I didn't understand the need to take him with us, except I had Eddie, and well, Malcolm had Hamish. I couldn't argue.

We trailed the water, close behind my werewolf. The sound of rushing water grew louder.

"The water's going to divide soon." I pointed to my right, through trees we couldn't see through.

"How do you know?" Malcolm asked.

"I can hear it."

Sure enough, the water split by rocks and a large sewer pipe drain. The distinctive smell of sulfur immediately rose through the grate. Eddie paused in his run to sniff the air and around the mud and rocks. He'd lost her scent.

"I'll go right, you head left." Malcolm pointed to the sewer as he cut across the running water in one easy stride and continued along its bank.

"Jerk." I glared at his retreating figure and then followed the ribbed metal pipe, trying to hear anything. Eddie followed behind me this time. I bent down and touched the metal. The vibrations of dripping, bugs, and running water ran under my hand. "She's too prissy to go down here," I said to Eddie and then stopped. Another vibration ran through my fingers. A rhythmic pounding. *Like someone running.*

Eddie released a low, guttural growl to get my attention. He repeated it again, his snout facing slightly to the left. The sewage had an extension.

I rolled my fingers in the air, cueing Eddie to turn to human form. He moved behind the tunnel and changed. When he stood, I ignored his nakedness and tossed him the small spare shorts I always carried with me. He slipped them on, his human body still fit and smooth.

Covered with leaves and vines, a set of bars gave us the entrance we needed. "Come on," I whispered. My thin, muscular frame quickly slipped through with the leather I wore. Eddie had a bit tougher time. Luckily for him, Malcolm had come back and easily separated the iron bars.

Moss and cobwebs covered the insides, along with who knew what else.

"Where's Hamish?" I asked him.

"Guarding the entrance." My eyes easily adjusted to the darkness inside the tunnel.

Malcolm chuckled. "I thought you said this chick was a naïve, little witch. You said we were supposed to come to Salem, do the job, and head back. Easy as pie."

I continued to look straight in front of me. "She's a lot more than I bargained for."

The tunnel forked into two directions.

"Let's split up again."

"Fine. Eddie, head back to the entrance to cover it with Hamish." I headed down the tubing where my gut told me Blair would have gone. Malcolm headed the other way. I sped my pace up and soon heard the sloshing of boots.

Blair slipped once, but the distinctive sploosh never followed. She must have caught herself. I knew I had her when I rounded a corner. She stood, her back to me and her chest heaving. She slowly turned around.

"Going somewhere?" My eyes burned with the thought of being this close to finishing the job. I ran my tongue over my pointed incisors and pulled my crossbow and arrow out, just in case she decided to try and make a run for it.

Blair's lilac eyes stared at the ground, her hands clenched and unclenched. Her eyes lost focus and her breathing grew ragged again. She was wearing a friggin' cocktail dress!

"Tsk. Tsk. Did your magic run out of steam?" The girl definitely had fight in her. "I thought you might be a bit of a challenge when I saw you sporting your fancy powers, but you're nothing more than an easy mark."

Blair glared at me, her nostrils flaring. Little bits of smoke and fire erupted from her fingers, and then fizzled out.

I laughed, setting my bow behind me again. "So predictable. You don't know how to use it, or pace out your energy." I shook my head and came closer. "You had one lousy teacher. You see, it's kind of like a marathon. You need to pace yourself, but instead, you put everything into that one tiny sprint. Any runner knows you can't win a marathon like that."

I jumped and grabbed her, throwing her hard against the wall. Chunks of algae and wall exploded everywhere. Blair barely landed when I was at her again. With one hand, I grabbed her fancy jacket collar and held her high in the air, her back against the jagged edge of the now-broken sewage tunnel.

She trembled beneath my hand. "You reek of vampire."

"I'll take that as a compliment. I'm full blooded. You, on the other hand, are a bloody inbred mix. Who activated you?"

"What?"

I tightened my grip on her throat. "I want to know who activated you because I wasn't filled in on this little, very critical detail. I hate walking blind into any situation."

"You studied me?"

I had to admit I admired this girl. Her life was moments from being snuffed and she spoke as if she were royalty. "That's what case files are for, chickie. I need to know my mark so I can think before he, or she, does."

She clenched her fists. "Why haven't you killed me?"

I huffed. My mistake, maybe she was dumb. "Haven't you been listening? I need to know who activated you."

"If I tell you, you'll k-kill m-me." Her voice wavered.

I shrugged, still holding her shirt collar. "You're dying one way or another. At least by me, I'll make it quick."

"You're the second person to promise me that tonight."

"Know one thing about me, I always keep my promises, and I *always* deliver. Now answer my question." I pulled my gun and pointed it at her heart. "I can start here, or here." I dropped the gun to her stomach.

"The witches 'activated' me."

"Your own clan?"

She nodded and a tear ran down her cheek.

"That's fucked."

"Tell me about it." She blew out a long breath. "My fiancé led me there."

Really? Her life has been severely jacked up. I didn't hold pity for anyone, but this girl? There was a fight in her, she just didn't know it yet. "Listen, I kinda like you. You're different than the others. Maybe it's the half vamp in you... I don't know." Her heart sped under my hand.

"Wait! If you originally planned on killing me, then how did you plan on getting my powers in the first place? And now that I have them, how will you get them?"

"That's my boss's problem." I tightened the grip on her shirt, knowing the girl had nothing more to share. My finger ran over an odd indentation on the skin of her neck. I pulled her collar to the side and gasped. "Where did that come from?" My voice thundered against the inside of the tunnel. I would need to act fast, Malcolm would soon be here.

"What?"

I brought her head close to mine. "The burn on the side of your neck."

She hesitated, so I bared my teeth and hissed at her, my incisors begging to bite her skin. "This could mean the difference between life and death for you. I'm not playing any games. Answer my question, damn it."

"N-Nobody knows. It must've happened when I was little. Why all the vamp drama?"

"Because I have the same mark!" I dropped her to the ground and pulled my leather collar aside. We stared at each other for a long moment. I inhaled and let the breath slowly out. "Who are your parents?"

Blair straightened her rumpled shirt. "I thought you read my case file."

"I know your mom got knocked up by an unknown vampire who dumped you after his precious wife died. He took you back to the witches so they could raise you. However, there were no names. I'm wondering if your father's name was left out intentionally. So I'm asking you nicely, who is your daddy?" My gut clenched in fear.

"Vlad Montour."

Everything froze. I stepped back and nearly stumbled on a wet rock. "That's my father, too."

Her jaw dropped. "Does that mean we're..."

"Son of a bitch," I whispered. "Half-sisters. I was sent to kill my own damn sister."

"Tori, who ordered this?"

I shook my head. There was no time to think. Malcolm would be here any moment, Eddie and Hamish were covering the main entrance. "It doesn't matter. You need to get away from here as fast as you can. As far away as possible. Don't ever try to reconnect with me. If you do, it'll be both our funerals." I could hear the panic in my own voice.

"What do you mean?"

"Every single supernatural creature is looking for you. I was told to take your dead body back so we could harness all the power you have. It's not like anything any immortal has ever seen. You hold unbelievable power that people will kill for."

"Where do I go?"

Anywhere! Just run! "You can't go back home. Your old life is in the past. You need to create a new identity and go into hiding. Don't even try to go back home to get precious belongings. Go!"

"I've never been alone before."

This girl needed to find herself and fast. She wouldn't make the week. "There's a first time for everything." I grinned sheepishly. "I'm letting you go. I've never lost a fight before." I pointed to the cracked opening in the tunnel. "Go through there. Malcolm's going to be here and I can't betray my own. I track down and kill your kind."

She made her way to the jagged opening.

"By the way, Blair?"

She turned to look at me, one leg already through the space. "Yeah?"

"Get a pair of sunglasses. Those purple eyes are going to mark you anywhere."

"I have brown eyes."

"Not anymore. The magic brewing inside you changed them."

"Unbelievable." She sighed, her eyes welling up. "I'm scared."

"You can do this."

"But I'm so complicated and flawed."

"Aren't we all?" I pointed to the opening. "Go! You're a survivor."

"Where?"

"Head to North Brother Island."

"Where's that?"

A growl echoed through the tunnel toward us. "New York. It's located in the East River just off the southeast end of the Bronx. Tell Wayne that Tori sent you. He owes me a favor."

Chapter 3

As Blair disappeared, I shot my gun down the corridor I knew was empty. I threw myself into the wall and fired again. Eddie barked wildly and soon appeared at my side, Malcolm right behind him.

"I'm okay." I pretended to be dazed. "The witch did some magic thing and threw me. She took off down that way." I faked a weak hand to point the opposite direction Blair had gone. Eddie sniffed the air, glanced at the jagged opening and back to me. He came over and nudged my shoulder. I sat up in the cold, shallow water. He looked at me again, as if in question, and nodding toward the entrance I pointed at, he finally understood. As if on cue he took off down the corridor barking. Malcolm was right after him running. I sat there dazed.

Unfortunately my dazed and confused state wasn't due to the magic I blamed it on, but rather the witch. She was my half-sister. Now I knew who she was, but so did someone else. Who would send me to kill my own sister? I had no idea why, but I planned on finding out who it was and why they deemed me the person to kill her.

I was a damn good hunter. I never missed my mark, but there were others who were good too. Why me? I slowly stood on my feet and brushed off my legs. I began the slow trot down the tunnel after Eddie and Malcolm. They were going to come back empty handed. I just hoped that I had played it out enough so they presumed she got away. It would be hard for Malcolm to believe I had lost her. I just had to use the surprise route. She had surprised me, and in more ways than one.

I finally caught up to a cursing Malcolm. "She's gone. Damn it! I knew I should've followed you. She wouldn't have been able to get the scoop on both of us. We'd have gotten her." He scuffed the tip of his boot on the dirt.

Turning, I followed him back to the entrance where Hamish now stood leaning against a tree. *Idiot*. Someone could have easily got the drop on him the way he was nonchalantly standing and gazing at the sky. It wasn't a Sunday afternoon picnic, for Pete's sake. We were on a witch hunt. That just showed how useless Hamish really was, but he made Malcolm happy, which in turn, made us happy.

Eddie came up beside me and rubbed against my leg. I would need to talk to him later. He would keep my secret no matter what. He owed me his life, and I knew he would do anything for me. He was more of a father figure to me than my dear ol' nut-job father.

There was no way I could lie to Eddie about what had happened back there. He knew which way the girl had really gone but had played it off for me. His nose was never wrong. I scratched behind his ear as he almost purred with delight. I laughed thinking that sometimes he was more of a lapdog or cat the way he went on when I caressed him.

Finally deeming it a lost cause, we decided to head back to the council. Besides, the sewer line that she had run into would branch out and come out at any one of fifteen locations in the city. Eddie was good but I convinced Malcolm that the hunt would take us a lot longer than we thought and we would be traveling throughout the whole city before we found her. Of course, I knew exactly where to go, seeing as I pointed her in the direction of Wayne. If he could keep his hands to himself, he would take care of her, or at least hide her and help get her out of there. Of course, deep down I knew that no matter what, she was doomed. She could get out of the city tomorrow and it wouldn't be good enough.

My dear little sister didn't know that once you had a target on your back it stayed there. It never went away, but rather grew with you. There was no way to get rid of it either, until the day you faced the maker.

Unless you could fight your way out of it. I saw firsthand the power she had inside of her and I could only hope that she had it in her to survive. There was nothing else I could do for her now. Yes. The rest of her life would be a fight. There was no way to stop that. I sighed as we began the trek home.

I paced by the window of my room, flipping my leather long cape behind me each time I turned. What would the council want now? It had been a week since the witch had gotten away and they hadn't given me another subject to hunt. It was unlike them, and it made me restless. Normally I had another assignment the next day. I was that good. This had been the first missed mark in over a decade.

They probably wanted me to stew on the failure. The council always got what they wanted. I swung toward the door as it opened.

Eddie, in human form, stood just outside the door. He always changed into his true form right before we arrived at the council if he went with me, which was very seldom. Although he was my wolf, he was still an outsider. The vampire coven decided long ago, when the random killings started, that the supernatural world was one that we would need to control.

The werewolves were a messy sort, along with the other different breeds of supernatural creatures. Werewolves are born into their breed. There is no bite or curse. The only way one can be a wolf is through blood. At least with the pack we'd been hunting for the last half century. We found out by trial (and many errors) the gene couldn't pass by a bite or through saliva. In order to trigger the curse they are born into, they must kill. After the age of sixteen the gene goes into effect, but stays dormant until their first kill.

Eddie was different. He didn't have the tendencies most werewolves had. I had never met another who could control the urges like he did. The urge to kill was more powerful in a werewolf, or other shape shifters, more than any other supernatural, or human. I'd trained Eddie, but his control was his alone to covet.

Many people didn't know werewolves were not the only shifters. There were many species. The list went on and on including snakes, lions and I had even heard of a group of crocodiles being shape shifters. I guess it made sense though. One animal was the same as the next. All a bunch of beasts to control.

I moved through the door he held open and made my way through the large building that housed the council meetings. Outside, it looked like a regular building. Inside, however, it looked like a medieval castle. The long hallway I walked down was simple, with cinderblock walls on both sides and old lanterns to light the way. The floor lay tiled with marble, the doors to each room made of solid antique wood. The old thick wood came from oak that at one time had been massive trees in some ancient forest.

I stared down, my short leather skirt showing more skin than most of the other vamps ever dared. I rather like my slight tan. It looked good against red, blood red. Except, of course, if that blood red was coming from a stake through the heart, or a beheading. That was just ugly... and dead. It also hurt like hell. So I'd heard, I never really got the chance to ask because all the vamps turned to ash and blew away before I could.

I came to the end of my hall and stood in the grand entrance that opened to other hallways and also the grand meeting room.

Lifting my chin, I pushed both doors open and stepped inside. I had no idea what was going on, but I did know the council wasn't happy. There had been something different about this hunt from the get-go. Why had the order been given to bring her back instead of kill her? It was a first for me, and I suddenly wanted to know why.

I forcefully pushed the door open and walked in. The council room reminded me of an old Louisiana courtroom. Supreme Court style. Eight men and women sat on the council, and all were present tonight. In front of where they sat were two desks with chairs behind them. The long bench where the council sat looked like judges for a case.

Staring into each one of the blue eyes, I strode across the long room toward the desks. Malcolm and Hamish sat behind a desk with their backs turned to me. Making sure my tall boots clicked loudly on the floor, I headed to the vacant desk with Eddie at my side.

"What's going on?" I asked and ignored the furious glares the council sent me.

"Victoria Montour and Malcolm Wilson, you've failed in your mission."

The head coven's words rang true. We had failed. I glanced over at Malcolm and knew he felt horribly disappointed. We never failed. I redirected my attention to the one speaking. One of the men directly below my father. He might as well have been a prince in line for the throne. Whatever he said went straight to my father and no one dared cross him.

"The mark was human. An easy target." He gestured to Eddie beside me. "Could the beast not catch her scent?"

"We lost it in water. I—"

"I'm not finished speaking!" Albert cut me off. Furious, he stared as his chest rose and fell. It was an old human habit, the man hadn't taken a proper breath in decades. "I'm not asking for clarification or an explanation."

His eyes bore into mine, skirting at the others in quick glances.

Instantly I understood why he didn't want to hear us out. He had known who she was. He had known from the start. *Why?*

Why did he send me after my own sister? The knowledge forced me to leave my expression emotionless and unreadable.

"I always believed you to be competent. I don't know what is causing you to become lax." Albert held up his slender hand, not wanting her to reply. "You've failed. It's unacceptable."

I could not hold back from answering. It had never been my strong point. "This is ridiculous! One mark gets away and you refuse to let me out. For a week! Now there's no chance of catching her!" My arms crossed over my chest and my right toe did the insistent tapping it liked to do when I was frustrated.

Albert frowned and purposely stared at my foot. "More than ample time to contemplate your mistakes before you return to the field. This was not acceptable." He glared at Malcolm and Hamish who quickly looked down. "You will *not* fail again." He turned back to me.

I hated my father. He made my life miserable. He was never around, but he made sure everything in my life was impossible. He was testing me. If he wanted me dead, I'd already be gone. Now I had to feign failure. "I won't," I mumbled.

"What did you say?" Albert pressed loudly. He was a vampire, he heard me loud and clear.

"It won't happen again." I punched each word out like a bullet, loud and sharp.

"Fine." He stacked his papers together against the antique wooden desk. "You'll be given your new marks. Come forward."

My head came up with a snap. *Marks?* I looked at Malcolm and we both made our way to the large desk. Hamish and Eddie stayed back, both obviously did not want to get close.

"You'll be given separate assignments. If you both take care of your next marks, then you can join back in the circle. If not, you'll be asked to leave."

We both knew what that meant. Exile. Forced to be turned into a renegade. We would become that which we hunted now. An enemy to the coven.

Nodding, we accepted the large brown envelopes handed to each of us.

Without another word I turned and strode out of the room. Malcolm would be sent to go after Blair. I was positive of that. Stomping down the halls, I headed back to my apartment room, slamming the door behind me and leaving Eddie, who had followed me, standing in the hall.

I dumped the contents of the package out and spread it on the bed. Everything I needed would be here. Whatever the coven knew about the mark – or everything they wanted me to know.

Everything down to the wire. The mark's natural being, their name, any information the government had on them, their criminal, medical, political history. Everything.

"Trent Alexander, what have you done to gain the dislike of the coven?" I sat down on the bed and stared at the information in the file, my eyes resting on the photos. One lay upside down. Picking it up, I turned it over and brought it closer to examine. Trent was a cutie with light brown hair and dark blue eyes. He looked out at the camera with a large smile.

"What is he?" Eddie asked from the other side of the door. He must've heard me mumble a moment ago.

"Werewolf." I rolled my eyes, not wanting to admit I was glad he had waited. "Come in."

Eddie came in and looked over my shoulder.

"He hasn't turned yet," I mentioned.

"You can tell?"

"Look at his eyes. You can tell he definitely hasn't."

"Really?" Eddie reached awkwardly for the photo, not completely sure what to do with human hands.

"That and the date in the bottom corner."

"What?" Eddie's eyebrows came up.

"File says he turned not long ago. That pic's from two years back."

I dropped my head down so my hair could cover my face and hide the smile sneaking through. Eddie scoffed but said nothing. I sorted through the rest of the photos, enjoying the handsome face, pushing it to memory. I went through the information one by one and read them to Eddie. Memorizing them to brain, we sat there for a couple hours making sure to get it all right.

Eddie whined and coughed to try and cover it.

"It's fine, Eddie." Other vamps hated Eddie, but they didn't understand his ability and loyalty. His size, his teeth and his poison terrified the others. Especially if they threatened me. He could kill a vampire if he had to. He just never did.

Confident we knew everything we needed, I stuffed the files and extra clothes into an overnight bag before heading down the hall to fill another bag with weapons.

Eddie disappeared to shift and meet me outside.

I wanted to get this mark out of the way fast so there would be no older coven pain in the arses breathing down my neck.

As I put knives, weapons, and guns into the large duffle bag, I thought about the mark. Trent Alexander lived in a small town called Luray, in the mountains of Virginia. It probably wouldn't be easy to find him. Having him already turned, he could easily slip into the mountains. Which would be hell trying to find him.

Outside, the cool spring air warned me of possible rain. Eddie stood waiting in the bed of my black truck. I unlocked the door and slipped inside. Trent was states away from me. It would take some time to get there as the coven was in the hidden mountains of Tennessee. These mountains I knew like the back of my hand, but the ones where I was going? Not so much. I could only hope I would be able to catch him without a run through the hills. If he turned out to be a brother, I would freakin' find my father and kill him myself.

I carried my mother's thin dagger sword. It was forged from ancient metal and blood. Always sharp, and deadly. That through his heart would stop his condescending nature toward his daughter – or should I say daughters now. Who knows how many others were out there?

Chapter 4

Hours later, just before sunrise, I parked at some off-name run-down motel. Checking in, I paid cash and ignored the gawking looks the owner gave me. It wouldn't bother me to add a few more spaces between his already missing teeth. He closed the office door quickly when Eddie poked his large wolf head through the door and walked with me to the last room on the right.

Inside the dimly lit room I pulled the papers out of the envelope one more time and studied them. When I was done I slipped into the small bathroom and pulled out my sterling, antique lighter. I watched as one by one the papers went up into flames. Sighing, I turned back and left the bathroom trash can smoldering. I closed the thick wool curtain to the tiny room and settled into a chair, my feet on the seventies style table beside it. I let Eddie rest on the bed as I played with the lighter, flicking it on and blowing it out as I waited for sundown.

I went over all the information now stored in my head. Trent became more and more a target, not a person. Eddie growled in his sleep, his paws running after someone or something. I watched him and wondered how many fights he and I had been through, and how many more there would be.

I checked my watch. Not much longer. First, I needed to find out where Trent was. *Probably work.* When the sun set, Eddie and I left the crap-motel and made our way to the grill in town that the files mentioned he worked at.

"Stay," I warned Eddie. He whined but hopped into the back bed of the truck and sat on his haunches. No one would come near the truck. He was a wolf, but could pass as one mean-looking dog. I glanced down at my clothes. Leather pants, black top, and the long leather jacket that looked like a cape from the back. Even in the heat, the clothes didn't bother me. The jacket hid the weapons strapped to my back. I probably wouldn't need them, but you never could be sure when it came to marks.

Sure enough, Trent was there busy bussing tables.

A waiter made his way to the booth beside mine and glanced my way. He stopped wiping the table and abruptly turned and walked away.

"What can I get you?"

Tearing my gaze from Trent, now behind the bar and glancing at me furiously, I looked up into a deep blue pair of eyes. They were remarkably dark, like sapphires. I had ocean blue eyes, what kind of creature could have eyes so blue? *What in the hell was wrong with me?* I didn't gaze into someone's eyes like that. I hunted. "Uh, beer... please." Trent still stood behind the bar, now playing bartender.

"Tap or bottle?"

"Whatever." I cleared my throat. "Tap... please."

He stood there smiling, and then must have realized he was staring as he visibly shook himself. "Kilkenny?"

I nodded, not caring what it was.

He finally turned to go get the drink. Trent stood behind the bar but didn't go near my waiter as he filled the pint glass. He came back carrying the frosted mug and set it in front of me. "Anything to eat?"

I could have eaten him at the moment. He smelled delicious. I ran my tongue over my lips. When was the last time I had fed directly off a human?

He stood waiting for me to answer.

The staring began to irritate the hell out of me. I was here on business, not pleasure. I shook my head more emphatically than I had meant to. "Nothing."

He nodded and walked away.

I couldn't help but admire the way his derriere filled out his jeans. If I had more time I might have thought about sticking around a few hours, or an extra day, to have some fun. Shrugging it off, I redirected my attention in the direction of the back door now swinging. *Crap!* I silently cursed at myself. I had been made and now the mark was skittish and scared as hell. He was going to run. Trent popped his head into view and looked straight at me.

I laid money on the table with the half empty mug and calmly made my way back outside. My cutie of a waiter was nowhere to be found. I moved to the rear exit and slipped outside. With vampire speed I pressed my back flat against the brick building. The sun's rays had left the bricks warm. Noise and whispered talking came from behind the end of the building. I crept soundlessly along the edge. A quick look, fast and observant, I peered around before settling back against the wall.

Trent stood there, but not on his own. Beside him was my sexy waiter. I crept as close to the edge without being detected. As I pulled a Glock from the holster on my hip, I realized I hadn't checked for weapons. Too distracted by the damn hottie. I shook my head, annoyed at myself.

"Three days, Evan," Trent whispered urgently. "You've got three days to find somewhere to go and hide. Where you won't hurt anyone like I did." He paused, probably looking around. "It's not safe here, buddy. You have to go. I told you not to get involved. I told you."

"What in the hell was I supposed to do?" Mr. Hottie didn't bother trying to keep his voice down. "Let them kill you, Trent? You're my damn brother."

Ah, hell. Now I knew why he looked so familiar. The hot waiter was the mark's brother. *Great.* Now I had two to deal with. By the way things were going, it wasn't going good for either brother. I shrugged. *Not my fault. I'm just doing my job.*

"Yes," Trent hissed. "We've known a long time what we were. When they killed mom and dad we understood we'd get the same fate if we triggered the damn curse. I'm your brother."

"I know you are!" Evan spat back.

The conversation always ended up the same. One mark would try to be the tough guy, the other played the smart one. It never ended well for either of them

"Evan, I promised to take care of you, not get you to trigger the damn curse! Now get out of here before the vamp finds us."

Evan obviously didn't know who I was. "Why? Why do you think I don't want to be a wolf? You've never asked. You think because I was fortunate enough to go to college, I deserve to run instead of you? Or is it because I'm younger and you think it's still your responsibility to take care of me?" Evan spat on the ground. "Well, it's not, Trent. I'm a grown ass man, and I'll do what we need to do to survive. You and I."

"You're just a kid."

Evan scoffed. "And you're not? You're just a pup."

What would their reaction be if I sent Eddie in? I knew I was eavesdropping instead of just killing, but I couldn't help myself. Their loyalty fascinated me.

"You need to go. Now." Evan sighed. "If that hot woman is a hunter like you think she is, she's on to us and you're screwed."

"I've got you to distract her." Trent made a sound that kept me from jumping out right then and attacking.

Evan must have glanced behind him to where I stood hidden behind the building. "She'll be here in a minute, maybe two. She didn't recognize me. She apparently doesn't know I killed that other hunter."

"Actually, I'm here now." I stepped from the side of the building as I spoke, guns pointed.

Both men looked up at me.

"Go! Now, Trent." Evan kept his voice low but I had no problem hearing it. They were crazy not to immediately try to run. They stood there, with my guns pointed at them, like sitting ducks.

"Yes, Trent. Try to run," I taunted.

A blur of action happened behind them that they didn't even notice. Almost didn't notice. Trent turned to glance behind him, but in the wrong direction. His head not moving fast enough for the vampire behind him.

A hunter. *Jason.* I knew him from meetings at the compound. Not a good sign. This hunter wasn't like the original ones, nor had he been trained the way I had. He was mean. I heard about the way he tortured beings before killing them. The council did not like him, but he was an asset. They needed him to do things others couldn't. The see no evil, hear no evil kind.

Jason's mouth pulled back in a sneer as he waited for Trent to make a move.

I had a feeling I'd been set up. Suddenly, I wanted the stupid werewolf to live.

Trent had nowhere to go. He wouldn't make it out of this alone.

I felt Eddie at my side. "Let it go, Jason. He's my mark." I angled the gun on Trent to Jason. There was a small gun hanging on my hip that carried ultraviolet bullets. I just couldn't grab it before Jason killed the mark, or he came after me. This was my kill. I needed it to get back in the good graces with the council.

"He's mine too, darlin'," Jason scoffed, giving me a blatant once over. "What did you think? The council wasn't going to send backup after your last epic failure? The great Victoria failed." He grinned maliciously, his canines pointed and ready. "I've grown so tired of hearing your damn name. When the job came up, I couldn't help but volunteer to take you down. What will your precious daddy say then?" His laugh echoed cruel and evil against the brick around us.

I glanced over at the two wolf brothers and realized they knew exactly who I was as well. Fear showed clearly in the older brother's eyes. He knew he wasn't making it out of this alive. Evan had a blank stare. Although younger, he obviously hid his emotions a lot better than his brother.

"Go home, Jason. I'm warning you. You don't want to make this between us."

Jason hissed. "I'm not going anywhere. Vlad, the ever-imposing daddy, always praising his precious daughter. The one who was a proper hunter."

I blinked in surprise. This was news to me. My father praising me? I highly doubted it. Another thought crossed my mind. Did all the hunters think of me this way? I pushed the thought aside. It didn't matter. Right now I needed to deal with the problem standing in front of me.

Jason clapped his hands. "It looks like I'm getting a bonus. Two weres and a vampire? And that stupid pet of yours. That always annoyed me as well. Why keep one of the shits we hunt?" He licked his lips. "I'll have to train that dog before I put it down."

My hand absently went to the top of Eddie's head as he growled at Jason. I knew exactly what Jason meant, so did Eddie.

- END OF EXCERPT -

Download it FREE

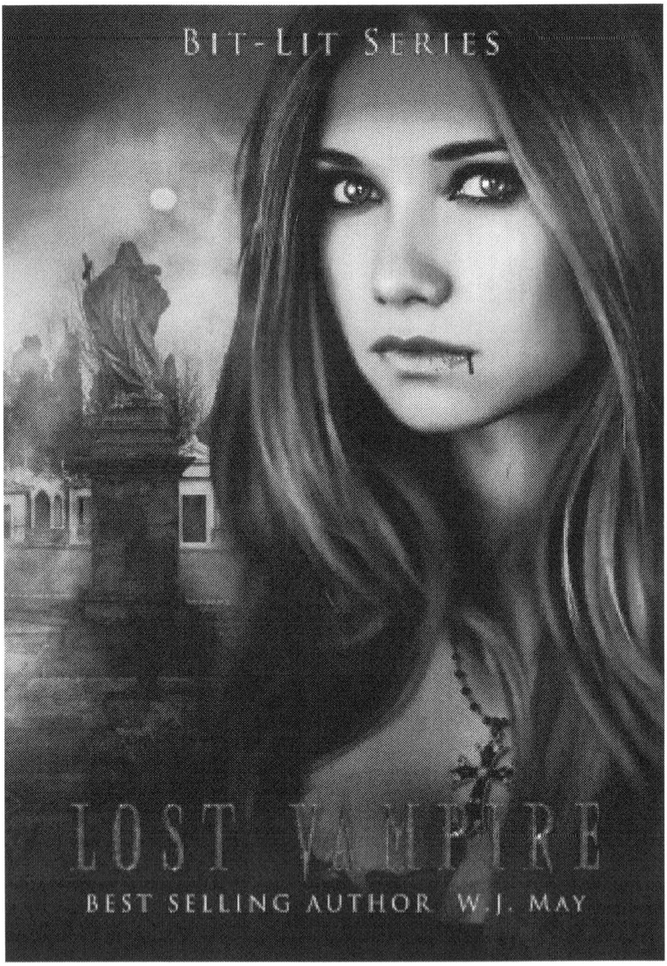
BIT-LIT SERIES
LOST VAMPIRE
BEST SELLING AUTHOR W.J. MAY

BIT-LIT SERIES PART II
COST OF BLOOD
BEST SELLING AUTHOR
W.J. MAY

BIT-LIT SERIES PART III
PRICE OF DEATH
BEST SELLING AUTHOR
W.J. MAY

Don't miss out!

Click the button below and you can sign up to receive emails whenever W.J. May publishes a new book. There's no charge and no obligation.

[Sign Me Up!](http://books2read.com/r/B-A-SSF-DHQH)

http://books2read.com/r/B-A-SSF-DHQH

BOOKS2READ

Connecting independent readers to independent writers.

Did you love *Lost Vampire*? Then you should read *Cost of Blood* by W.J. May!

From Bestselling Fantasy/Paranormal author, W.J. May comes a new kind of vampire shifter series. Get ready to be blown away!

Lost Vampire Book 1 of the Bit-Lit Series is FREE

The future is not a safe place.

Fleeing the Archon Jeremiah's rage and his purge of Brooklyn, the vampire Tay Maslov has sought aid from neighbouring Archon Bethania of Manhattan, decadent, nihilistic Bethania. The forever-young makes a deal with the young Feral; be her spy and all will be well. Perhaps she will even regain her place at an Archon's unholy side. But with the Shadow War between the Shifters and the Elders heating up, Kaiden and Tay find themselves dragged into a twisting game of play and counter-play, as the different factions threaten to tear the city apart...

Book 1 - Lost Vampire
Book 2 - Cost of Blood
Book 3 - Price of Blood - Coming in January 2016

Also by W.J. May

Bit-Lit Series
Lost Vampire
Cost of Blood

Blood Red Series
Courage Runs Red
The Night Watch

Daughters of Darkness: Victoria's Journey
Huntress
Coveted (A Vampire & Paranormal Romance)
Victoria

Hidden Secrets Saga
Seventh Mark - Part 1
Seventh Mark - Part 2
Marked By Destiny
Compelled
Fate's Intervention
Chosen Three

The Chronicles of Kerrigan
Rae of Hope
Dark Nebula
House of Cards
Royal Tea
Under Fire
End in Sight

The Hidden Secrets Saga

Seventh Mark (part 1 & 2)

The Senseless Series
Radium Halos
Radium Halos - Part 2
Nonsense

Standalone
Shadow of Doubt (Part 1 & 2)
Five Shades of Fantasy
Glow - A Young Adult Fantasy Sampler
Shadow of Doubt - Part 2
Four and a Half Shades of Fantasy
Full Moon
Dream Fighter
What Creeps in the Night
Forest of the Forbidden
HuNted
Arcane Forest: A Fantasy Anthology
Ancient Blood of the Vampire and Werewolf

Printed in Great Britain
by Amazon